The Secret Child
&
The Cowboy CEO

JANICE
MAYNARD

MILLS
BOON

First published in Great Britain 2011
by Mills & Boon, an imprint of Harlequin (UK) Limited,
Large Print edition 2011
Eton House, 18-24 Paradise Road,
Richmond, Surrey TW9 1SR

© Janice Maynard 2010

ISBN: 978 0 263 22367 5

Harlequin (UK) policy is to use papers that are natural,
renewable and recyclable products and made from
wood grown in sustainable forests. The logging
and manufacturing process conform to the legal
environmental regulations of the country of origin.

Printed and bound in Great Britain
by CPI Antony Rowe, Chippenham, Wiltshire

JANICE MAYNARD

came to writing early in life. When her short story *The Princess and the Robbers* won a red ribbon in her third-grade school arts fair, Janice was hooked. She holds a B.A. from Emory and Henry College and an M.A. from East Tennessee State University. In 2002 Janice left a fifteen-year career as an elementary teacher to pursue writing full-time. Her first love is creating sexy, character-driven, contemporary romance. She has written for Kensington and NAL, and now is so very happy to also be part of the Mills & Boon® family— a lifelong dream, by the way!

Janice and her husband live in beautiful east Tennessee in the shadow of the Great Smoky Mountains. She loves to travel and enjoys using those experiences as settings for books.

Hearing from readers is one of the best perks of the job! Visit her website at www.janicemaynard.com or email her at JESM13@aol.com. Snail mail is P.O. Box 4611, Johnson City, TN 37602, USA. And of course, don't forget Facebook (www.facebook.com/janiceSmaynard) and MySpace (www.myspace.com/janicemaynard).

For Caroline and Anna,
who shared with us
one wonderful Wyoming summer.
A van, an X-cargo and the
open road…six weeks of fun…
memories to last a lifetime.

One

A half-dozen years... One look from those fabulous eyes and she could still make him act like a foolish kid.

Trent felt his heart slug hard in his chest. Oxygen backed up in his lungs. *Dear God, Bryn.*

He dragged the remnants of his self-control together and cleared his throat, pretending to ignore the woman standing beside his father's bed.

Her presence in the room made him sweat.

The lust, loathing and sharp anger teeming in his gut made it impossible to act naturally, particularly since he wasn't sure if the anger was self-directed or not.

His father, Mac, watched them both with avid curiosity, giving his son a canny, calculating look. "Aren't you going to say something to Bryn?"

Trent tossed aside the damp towel he'd been using to dry his hair when he walked into the room. He folded his arms across his bare chest, then changed his mind and slid his hands into his back pockets. He turned toward the silent woman with what he hoped like hell was an impassive expression. "Hello, Bryn. Long time no see."

The insolence in his tone caused a visible wince to mark her otherwise serene expression, but she recovered rapidly. Her eyes were as cool as a crisp Wyoming morning. "Trent." She inclined her head stiffly in a semblance of courtesy.

For the first time in weeks, Trent saw anticipation on his father's face. The old man was pale
and weak, but his voice was strong. "Bryn's
here to keep me company for the next month.
Surely she won't aggravate me like all those
other cows. I can't stand strangers poking and
prodding at me...." His voice trailed off, slur-
ring the last few words.

Trent frowned in concern. "I thought you
said you didn't need a nurse anymore. And the
doctor agreed."

Mac grunted. "I don't. Can't a man invite an
old friend without getting cross-examined? Last
time I checked, this was *my* ranch."

Trent smothered a small, reluctant grin. His
father was a grouch on his best days, and re-
cently, he'd turned into Attila the Hun. Three
nurses had quit, and Mac had fired two more.
Physically, the Sinclair patriarch might be on
the mend, but he was still mentally fragile.

It was a comfort to Trent that, although exhaustion marked Mac's face, he was as ornery as

ever. The heart attack he'd suffered two months ago, when his youngest son was found dead of a heroin overdose, had nearly cost the family *two* lives.

Bryn Matthews spoke up. "I was happy to come when Mac contacted me. I've missed you all."

Trent's spine stiffened. Was that a taunt in her perfectly polite words?

He forced himself to look at her. When she was barely eighteen, her beauty had tugged at him like a raw ache. But he'd been on the fast track already, an ambitious twenty-three-year-old with no time for a young wife.

She had matured into a lovely woman. Her skin was the same sun-kissed ivory. Her delicate features were framed by a thick fall of shiny black hair. And her almost-violet eyes gazed at him warily. She didn't appear unduly surprised to see him, but he was shocked right down to his bare toes. His heart was beating so hard, he was afraid she'd be able to see the evidence with her own eyes.

She was dressed more formally than he had ever seen her, in a dark pantsuit with a prim white blouse beneath. Her waist was narrow, her hips curvy. The no-nonsense cut of her jacket disguised her breasts, but his imagination filled in the details.

Bitterness choked him. Bryn was here to cause trouble. He knew it. And all he could think about was how badly he wanted her in his bed.

He ground his teeth together and lowered his voice. "Step into the hall with me." He didn't phrase it as a request.

Bryn preceded him from the room and turned to face him across the narrow space. They were so close he could see a pulse beating in the side of her throat. And he caught a whiff of her familiar, floral-scented perfume. Delicate…like she was. The top of her head barely came up to his chin.

He ignored the arousal jittering through his veins. "What in the hell are you doing here?"

Her eyes flared in shock. "You know why. Your father asked me to come."

Trent growled low in his throat, wanting to pound a hole in the wall. "If he did, it was because you manipulated him into thinking it was his idea. My brother Jesse's not even cold in his grave and yet here you are, ready to see what you can get."

Her eyes flashed, reminding him she had never lacked for gumption. "You're a self-righteous ass," she hissed.

"Never mind." He cut her off, swamped with a wave of self-loathing. She was a liar. And she had tried to blame Jesse for another man's sins. But that didn't stop Trent from wanting her.

He firmed his jaw. "Apparently you couldn't be bothered to make it to the funeral?"

Her lips trembled briefly. "No one let me know that Jesse had died until it was too late."

"Convenient." He sneered. Only by whipping up his anger could he keep his hands off her.

The hurt that flickered in her gaze made him feel as if he was kicking a defenseless puppy. At one time he and Bryn had been good friends. And later—well…there had been a tantalizing hint of something more. Something that might have developed into a physical relationship, if he hadn't screwed things up.

Bryn had been innocent, not-quite-eighteen, and Trent had freaked out over his reaction to her. He had rejected her clumsily when she asked him to be her date for the senior prom, and she was heartbroken. A few weeks later, she and Jesse started dating.

Had Bryn done it to hurt him?

Trent couldn't blame Jesse. Jesse and Bryn were the same age and had a lot in common.

Bryn's face was pale. Her body language said she wanted to be anywhere other than in this hallway with him.

Well, that was too damn bad.

He leaned forward to tuck a strand of her hair behind her ear, whispering softly, "If you think I'll let you take advantage of a sick old man, you're an idiot." He couldn't stop himself.

Bryn's chin lifted and she stepped sideways. "I don't care what you think about me, Trent. I'm here to help Mac. That's all you need to know. And I'm sure you'll be on your way back to Denver very soon…right?" In another situation the naked hope on her face would have amused him. But at the moment, he couldn't escape the irony.

He cocked his head, wishing he could discern the truth. Why had she really come back to Wyoming?

He shrugged. "Tough luck, Bryn. I'm here for the foreseeable future.… I got tapped to take a turn running the place until the old man is back on his feet. So you're stuck with me, sweetheart."

Her cheeks flushed, and her air of sophistication vanished like mist in the morning sun. For the first time he saw a hint of the girl she had been at eighteen. Her agitation made him want to soothe her when what he should be doing was showing her the door.

But his good sense was at odds with his libido. He wanted to crush her mouth beneath his, strip away the somber-looking jacket and find the curves he would map in detail.

The past beckoned, sharp and sweet.... He remembered one of the last times he and Bryn had been together before everything went so badly wrong. He had flown in for his dad's birthday party. Bryn had run to meet him, talking a mile a minute as soon as he got out of the car. She was all legs and slim energy. And she'd had a crush on him.

She would have been mortified if she'd realized he had known all along. So, on that long-ago day he had treated her with the same easy camaraderie that had always existed between them. And he'd done his best to ignore the tug of attraction he felt.

They were not a match in any way.

At least that's what he'd told himself.

Now, in this quiet hallway, he got lost for a moment, caught between the past and the present. He touched her cheek. It was soft…warm. Her eyes were the color of dried lavender, like the small bouquets his mother used to hang in the closets. "Bryn." He felt the muscles in his throat tighten.

Her gaze was guarded, her thoughts a mystery. No longer did he see naked adoration on her face. He didn't trust her momentary docility. She might be trying to play him for her own advantage. But she'd soon find that she was no match for him. He'd do anything to protect his father. Even if it meant bedding the enemy to learn her secrets.

Without thought or reason, his lips found hers. Their mouths clung, pressed, moved awkwardly. His hands found the ripe curves of her breasts and he caressed her gently. He thought she responded, but he couldn't be sure. He was caught up in some weird time warp. When sharp daggers of arousal made him breathless, he jerked back, drawing great gulps of air into his starving lungs.

He ran his hands through his hair. "No." He couldn't think of a follow-up explanation. Was he talking to her or himself?

Bryn's face was dead-white but for two spots of hectic color on her cheekbones. She wiped a shaky hand across her mouth and backed away from him.

Distress filled her eyes and embarrassment etched her face.

She turned and walked away, her gait jerky.

He watched her go, his gut a knot the size of Texas. If she had come again to try to convince them that Jesse had fathered her child, she would get short shrift. It would be in extremely bad taste to accuse a man who wasn't here to defend himself.

Remembering Jesse at this particular moment was a mistake. It brought back every single moment of torment Trent had experienced when his baby brother started dating the woman Trent wanted. The situation had been intolerable, and only by keeping himself in Denver, far away from temptation, had Trent been able to deal with it.

But in his heated fantasies, during the dead of night, it was Bryn, always Bryn. He'd told himself he was over her. He'd told himself he hated her.

But it was all a lie....

Bryn didn't have the luxury of locking herself in her room and giving way to the storm of emotions that tightened her throat and knotted the muscles between her shoulder blades. Why couldn't Mac's son Gage have been here...or Sloan? She loved both of them like brothers and would have been happy for a reunion. But Trent... Oh, God, had she given herself away? Did he know now she had never gotten over her fascination with him?

She couldn't allow herself to think about what had just happened…refused to acknowledge how she enjoyed the way his hard, naked chest felt beneath her hands. Had she pushed him away or leaned into him?

Don't be a fool, Bryn. Nothing can come of going down that road but more hurt.

When Bryn was sure Mac was napping, she went out to the car to retrieve her suitcase and carry-on. Trent had disappeared to do chores. Bryn was grateful for the respite from his presence.

She stood, arms upraised, and stretched for a moment, shaking off the stiffness from the long flight and subsequent drive. She had forgotten the clearness of the air, the pure blue of the Wyoming sky. In the distance, the Grand Tetons ripped at the heavens, their jagged peaks still snow-capped, even in mid-May.

Despite her stress and confusion, after six years of exile, the familiar Crooked S brand entwined prominently in the massive wrought-iron gates at the end of the driveway felt like a homecoming. The imposing metalwork arched skyward as if to remind importunate visitors, "You're nobody. Trespass at your own risk."

The four boys used to call it the "Crooked Ass Ranch." Mac hadn't thought the irreverence funny.

Before going back inside, Bryn studied the house with yearning eyes. Little had changed since she had been gone. The sprawling two-story structure of timber and stone had cost millions to build, even in the mid-seventies when Mac had constructed it for his young bride.

The house rested, like a conqueror, on the crest of a low hill. Everything about it reeked of money, from the enormous wraparound porch to the copper guttering that gleamed in the midday sun. The support beams for the porch were thick tree trunks stripped of bark. Flowering shrubs tucked at the base of the house gave a semblance of softness to the curb appeal, but Bryn wasn't fooled.

This was a house of powerful, arrogant men.

Back inside, she picked up her phone and dialed her aunt's number. Even though the Sinclair's ranch was in the middle of nowhere, Mac had long ago paid for a cell tower to be built near the house. With enough money, anything could be bought, including all the trappings of an electronic society.

When Aunt Beverly answered, Bryn felt immediately soothed by the familiar voice. Six years ago her mother's older sister had taken in a scared, pregnant teenager and had not only helped Bryn enroll in community college and find a part-time job, but when the time came, she had also been a doting grandmother, in every sense of the word, to Allen.

Bryn chatted with a cheer she didn't feel, and then asked to speak to her son. Allen's tolerance for phone conversations was limited, but it comforted Bryn to hear his high-pitched voice. The family next door had two new puppies. Aunt

Beverly was taking him to the neighborhood pool tomorrow. His favorite toy fire truck had lost a wheel. "Love you. Bye, Mommy."

And with that, he was gone.

Beverly came back on the line. "Are you sure everything is okay, sweetheart? He can't make you stay."

Bryn squeezed the bridge of her nose and cleared her throat. "I'm fine…honestly. Mac is weaker than I expected, and they're grieving for Jesse."

"What about you?"

Bryn paused, trying to sort through her chaotic feelings. "I'm still coming to terms with it. He didn't break my heart. What we had was more hormones than happily-ever-afters. But he nearly destroyed my world. I never forgave him for that, but I didn't want him dead." Her throat thickened, making it hard to speak.

Beverly's gentle words echoed her strength. "We've gotten by without the money all this time, Bryn. It's not worth losing your pride and your self-respect. If they give you trouble, promise me you'll leave."

Bryn smiled, though her aunt couldn't see her. "Allen deserves a share of the wealth. And I'll put it in a special account for his college education and whatever else he might need down the road. It will give him a secure future, and that's important. I'll be home in four weeks. Don't you worry about me."

They chitchatted a few more minutes, but then Allen demanded Aunt Beverly's attention. Bryn clicked the phone shut and blinked rapidly to stave off a wave of loneliness and heartache. She had never been away from her baby more than a night or two.

Allen would be fine. She knew that. But she felt like she'd been given a life sentence without parole.

She changed into comfortable jeans and a petal-pink sweater. It was time to check on Mac.

She tiptoed as she neared his room. He needed

his rest desperately. Fortunately, this entire wing of the house was quiet as a tomb, so maybe he was still sleeping. Everything in his luxurious but masculine suite was designed for comfort, so as long as his medication was relieving any pain, he should be recovering on schedule.

But she knew as well as anyone that grief manifested itself in serious and complex ways.

Her foot was moving forward to enter the room when she realized Trent was sitting on the side of his father's bed. She caught her breath and drew back instinctively.

Trent murmured softly, the conversation one-sided as Mac slept. Bryn couldn't make out the words. Trent stroked his father's forehead, the gesture so gentle a huge lump strangled her throat.

The old man was feeble and frail in the large bed. His eldest son, in contrast, was virile, strong and healthy. Seeing Trent show such tenderness shocked her. He had always been a reserved man, self-contained and difficult to read. Striking and impressive, but a man of few smiles.

His steel-gray eyes and jet-black hair, dusted with premature silver at the temples, complemented a complexion tanned dark by the sun. Despite the years he'd been gone from Wyoming, he still retained the look of one who spent much of his time outdoors.

She swallowed hard and forced herself to enter the room. "When is his next doctor's appointment?"

Though her words were soft and low, Trent snatched back his hand and rose to his feet, his expression closed and forbidding. "Next Tuesday, I think. It's written on the kitchen calendar."

She nodded, her voice threatening to fail her. "Okay." She tried to step past him, but he put a hand on her arm.

Trent was raw with grief over the loss of his brother. He could barely contemplate the possibility of losing the old man so soon after Jesse's death. How could Bryn still turn him inside out? His grip tightened. Not enough to hurt her, but enough to let her know he wouldn't be a pushover.

He put his face close to hers, perhaps to prove to himself that kissing her was a temptation he could withstand. "Stay out of my way, Bryn Matthews. And we'll get along just fine."

This close he could see the almost imperceptible lines at the corners of her eyes. She was not a child anymore. She was a grown woman. And he saw in one brief instant that she had suffered, too.

But then she blinked and the tense moment was gone. "No problem," she said, her voice quiet so as not to wake her patient. "You won't even know I'm here."

Trent strode outdoors blindly, feeling suffocated and out of control. He needed physical exertion to clear his head. A half hour later, he slung a heavy saddle over the corral rail and wiped sweat from his forehead. Working out at the gym in Denver wasn't quite the same as doing ranch labor. The chores here were hard, hot and strangely cathartic. It had been a decade since Trent had played an active role in running the Crooked S. But the skills, rusty as they might be, were coming back to him.

He had repaired fences, mucked out stalls, hunted down stray calves and helped the vet deliver two new foals. Up until yesterday, his brothers, Gage and Sloan, had done their part, as well. But they were gone now—for at least a month—until one of them returned to relieve Trent.

A month seemed like a lifetime.

Trent's father employed an army of ranch hands, but in his old age, he'd become cantankerous and intolerant of strangers—reluctant to let outsiders know his business. He'd fired his foreman not long before Jesse's death. The tragedy had taken a toll on all of them, but Mac had aged overnight.

Even now, eight weeks after Jesse's death, Trent was blindsided at least once a day by a poignant memory of his youngest brother. The coroner's report still made no sense. Cause of death: heroin overdose. It was ridiculous. Jesse had been an Eagle Scout, for God's sake. Had someone slipped him the drug without his knowledge?

Trent finished rubbing down the stallion and glanced at his watch. He'd fallen into the habit of checking on the old man at least once an hour, and with Bryn around, that routine was more important than ever. He didn't trust her one damn bit. Six years ago she had lied to weasel her way into the family. Now she was back to try again. The next few weeks were going to be hell.

Especially if he couldn't keep his traitorous body under control.

Two

When Trent stormed out of the room, albeit quietly, Bryn couldn't decide if she was disappointed or relieved. He made her furious, but at the same time, she felt so alive when he was around. Six years had not changed that.

She sat at Mac's bedside for a half hour, just watching the rise and fall of his chest. In some ways, it was as if no time had passed at all. This man had meant the world to her.

When he finally roused from his nap and shifted upright in the bed, she handed him a tumbler of water, which he drained thirstily and placed on the bedside table.

He stared at her, his expression sober. "Do you hate me, girl?"

She shrugged, opting for honesty. "I did for a long time. You broke your promise to me." When her parents, Mac's foreman and cook, died in a car accident years ago, Mac had sat a fourteen-year-old Bryn down in his study and promised her that she would always have a home on the huge Wyoming ranch where she had grown up.

But four years later that promise was worth less than nothing. Jesse, spoiled golden child and chillingly proficient liar, turned them all against her in one insane, surreal instant.

Mac shifted in the bed. "I did what I had to do." His words were sulky…pure, stubborn Mac. But knowing how much he had suffered softened Bryn's heart a little.

In spite of herself, forgiveness tightened her throat and squeezed her chest. Mac had made a mistake.... They all had made mistakes, Bryn included. But Mac had done his best to look out for her after her parents were gone. Until it all went to hell.

Then he'd sent her to Aunt Beverly. Punishment by exile. Bryn had been crushed. But six years was a long time to hold a grudge.

She sighed. "I'm sorry Jesse died, Mac. I know how much you loved him."

"I loved you, too," he said gruffly, not meeting her eyes.

His behavior bore that out. Mac hadn't forgotten her. For six years he'd sent birthday and Christmas presents like clockwork. But Bryn, hugging her injured pride like the baby she was, promptly sent them back every time.

Now shame choked her. Did Mac's one moment of weakness erase all the years he'd been like a grandfather to her?

She took a deep breath. "I came back to Wyoming because you asked me to. But even if you hadn't, I would have been here once I

30   THE SECRET CHILD & THE COWBOY CEO

knew Jesse was gone. We have to talk about a lot of things, Mac." Like the fact that she wanted a paternity test to prove that Jesse was Allen's father. And that her son was entitled to his dead father's share of the Sinclair empire.

Mac's lips trembled, and he pulled the blanket to his chest. "There's time. Don't push it, girl." He slid back down in the bed and closed his eyes, effectively ending the conversation.

Bryn stepped into the hall, leaving the bedroom door open so she could hear him call out if he needed her. The study was only steps away. She couldn't help herself...she went in.

The room seemed benign now, not at all the way she remembered it in her nightmares. That dreadful day was etched in her memory by the sharp blades of hurt and disillusionment. She'd considered herself an honorary Sinclair, but they had sided with Jesse.

"What are you doing in here?"

Trent's sharp voice startled her so badly, she spun and almost lost her balance. She placed a steadying hand on the rolltop desk and bit her lip. "You scared me."

His scowl deepened. "I asked you a question, Bryn."

She licked her lips, her legs like jelly. "I wanted to send my son an e-mail."

Trent's face went blank, but she saw him clench his fists. "Don't mention your son in my presence," he said, his voice soft but deadly. "Not if you know what's good for you."

Bryn could take the knocks life dealt her, but no one was going to speak ill of her baby while there was breath in her body.

She squared her shoulders. "His name is Allen. And he's Jesse's son. I know it, and I think deep in your heart, you and Mac and Gage and Sloan know it, too. Why would I lie, for heaven's sake?"

Trent shrugged, his gaze watchful. "Women lie," he said, his words deliberately cutting, "all the time—to get what they want."

For the first time, she understood something

that had never before been clear to her, especially not as an immature teenager. When Mac's flighty young wife abandoned her family years ago, the damage had run deep.

The Matthews family had come along to fill in the gaps. For more than a decade, Bryn and her mother had been the only females in an all-male enclave. And Bryn had assumed that trust was a two-way street. But when Jesse swore that he had never slept with Bryn, Mac and Trent had believed him. It was as simple as that.

Bryn chose her words carefully. "I don't lie. Maybe you've had bad luck with the women in your life, but I can't help that. I told the truth six years ago, and I'm telling the truth now."

He curled his lip. "Easy for you to say. With Jesse not here to defend himself."

She tamped down her anger, desperate to get through to him. "Jesse was a troubled boy who grew into a troubled man. You all spoiled him and babied him, and he used your love as a weapon. I have the scars to prove it. But

Jesse's gone, and I'm still here. And so is my son. He deserves to know his birthright—his family."

Trent leaned back against his wall, the hard planes of his face showing no signs of remorse. "How much do you want?" he said bluntly. "How big a check do I have to write to make you leave and never come back?"

The bottom fell out of her stomach, and her jaw actually dropped. "Go to hell," she said, her lips trembling.

He grabbed her wrist as she headed for the door. "Maybe I'll take you with me," he muttered.

This time, there was no pretense of tenderness. He was angry and it showed in his kiss. Their mouths battled, his hands buried in her hair, hers clenched on his shoulders.

At eighteen she'd thought she understood sex and desire. After Jesse's betrayal, she'd understood that his love was an illusion. As was Mac's…and Trent's.

Now, with six years of celibacy to her credit and a heart that was being split wide open with the knowledge that she had never stopped loving Trent Sinclair, she was lost.

The kiss changed in one indefinable instant. She curled a hand behind his neck, stroking the short, soft hair that was never allowed to brush his collar. His skin was warm, so warm.

She went limp in his embrace, too tired to fight anymore. Her breasts were crushed against his hard chest. Her lips no longer struggled with his. She capitulated to the sweetness of being close to him again. A sweetness tainted with the knowledge that he thought she was a liar. That she had tried to manipulate them all.

Gradually, they stepped away from a dangerous point of no return. Trent's expression was closed, his body language defensive.

She nodded jerkily toward the desk. "I'll use the computer later. I'm sure you have work to do."

When he didn't respond at all, she fled.

* * *

Trent was not accustomed to second-guessing himself. Confidence and determination had propelled him to success in the cutting-edge, fast-paced world of solar and wind energy. When he'd received the call about his father's heart attack, Trent had been in the midst of an enormous deal that involved buying up a half-dozen smaller companies and incorporating them into the already well-respected business model that was Sinclair Synergies.

Except for some start-up cash that had long since been repaid, he'd never relied on his father's money. Trent was damned good at what he did. So why was the CEO of said company cooling his heels in Wyoming shoveling literal horseshit?

And why in the hell couldn't he read the truth in a woman's eyes? A woman who had stayed in his heart all these years like a bad case of indigestion.

Had Jesse lied? And if so, why? Mac, Sloan,

Gage and Trent had doted on the little boy who came along three years after his one-after-the-other siblings. Jesse had suffered from terrible bouts of asthma, and the entire family rallied whenever he was sick. So, yeah—maybe Bryn was right. Maybe they *had* catered to Jesse's whims, especially when their mother bailed on them. But that didn't mean Jesse was a bad person.

Heroin overdose. Trent shifted uneasily in Mac's office chair. Going through the books was proving to be more difficult than he'd anticipated. Jesse had never been a whiz at math, so God knows why Mac put him in charge of the finances. His youth alone should have been a red flag. And his inexperience.

Already, Trent was uneasy about some ways money had been shifted from one account to another. A heart-to-heart with Mac was in order, but until the old man was a little steadier on his emotional feet, Trent would hold off on the questions.

Which brought him back to Bryn. What was Mac thinking? Why had he brought Bryn back to Wyoming?

Trent shoved back from the desk and stood up to stretch, his eyes going automatically to the magnificent scene outside the window. Wyoming was his birthplace, his home. And he loved it. But it had not been able to hold him… or Gage or Sloan, either, for that matter.

Gage had developed a bad case of wanderlust at an early age…and Sloan—well—Sloan's brilliance was never going to be challenged by ranching. Had Jesse felt the need to be his father's heir apparent? It didn't fit what Trent knew of his baby brother's temperament, but what else could explain Jesse's role in running the ranch?

At one time the Crooked S had been the largest cattle operation in a six-state area…back when Mac was in his forties and had a brand-new twenty-year-old bride at his side. Now it was nothing more than acres of really valuable land.

What would become of the ranch when Mac was gone?

Trent waited until he heard Bryn talking on the phone in her bedroom before he went back in to check on his dad. Mac was sitting up in bed, and already his eyes seemed brighter, his skin a healthier shade. Had something as simple as bringing Bryn home wrought the change?

Trent sat down in a ladderback chair near the foot of the bed and hooked one ankle over the opposite knee. He put his hands behind his head and leaned back. "You're looking better."

Mac grunted. "I'll live." The two of them had never been much for sentimentality.

Trent smothered a smile. "Do you feel like going for a ride? I need to pick up a few things in town. Might do you good to get out for a couple of hours."

His father seemed to wilt suddenly, as though his burst of energy had come and gone in an instant. "Don't think I ought to try it yet. But maybe Bryn would like to go."

Trent stiffened. He wasn't ready to spend the hour and a half it would take to go into Jackson Hole and back cooped up in a car with the woman who was tying him in knots. "I'd say she's still tired from her trip. And I can be there and back in no time."

Mac's dark eyes, so much like his son's, held a calculating gleam. "Bryn promised to pick out a new blanket for my bed at the Pendleton store. You know how women are…always shopping for something. I don't want to disappoint her. And you can have dinner before you drive back. Julio and I are going to play poker tonight."

Julio was one of the ranch hands. Trent sighed. He knew when he'd been suckered. But he wasn't going to fight with his dad…not yet.

Moments later, Trent knocked on Bryn's door. It was slightly ajar, and he waited impatiently until she finished her phone conversation.

* * *

Bryn ground her teeth when she realized Trent was standing in the doorway. Maybe she should put a cow bell on him so he'd quit sneaking up on her. "What do you want?" The curt question was rude, but she was still stinging from their earlier encounter.

Trent's expression was no happier than hers. His lips twisted. "I'm supposed to take you into town with me to do some errands…a blanket my father mentioned? And he wants me to take you out to dinner."

She cocked her head, reading his discomfort in every taut muscle of his lean body. "And you'd rather wrestle with a rattlesnake…right?"

He shrugged, leaning against the door frame, his face impassive. "I'm here this month to make my father's life easier. And if that means allowing him to boss me around, I'm willing to do so."

"Such a dutiful son," she mocked.

His jaw hardened. "Be out front in twenty minutes."

Bryn fumed as he walked out on her, and she locked her door long enough to change from jeans into nice dress slacks and a spring sweater. She didn't understand Trent at all. But she read his hostility loud and clear. From now on, there would be no kissing, no reliving the past. She was here to right past wrongs, and Trent was no more than a minor inconvenience.

She managed to make herself believe that until she climbed into the passenger seat of a silver, high-end Mercedes and got a whiff of freshly showered male and expensive aftershave. *Oh, Lord.*

Her stomach flipped once…hard…and she clasped her hands in her lap, her feet planted on the floor and her spine plumb-line straight.

The atmosphere in the car was as frigid as a January Wyoming morning. Trent turned the satellite radio to a news station, and they managed to complete the entire journey in total silence.

He let her out in front of the Pendleton store. "I've got some business to attend to. Can you entertain yourself for an hour or so?"

She sketched a salute. "Yes, sir. I'll be right here at six o'clock."

His jaw went even harder than before, and his tires squealed as he pulled away from the curb.

Bryn's brief show of defiance drained away, and her bottom lip trembled. Why couldn't Trent let the past stay in the past? Why couldn't they start over as friends?

She picked out Mac's beautiful Native American–patterned blanket in no time, and visited a few more of the shops down the street, managing to select gifts for her aunt and for Allen. A friendly shopkeeper offered to stow Bryn's bulky packages until Trent returned, so Bryn took the opportunity to stretch her legs.

Back in Minnesota she and Beverly and Allen

walked each evening when the weather was nice. The two women enjoyed the exercise, and it was good for Allen to use up some of his energy before bedtime.

Bryn missed her baby. He hated it when she called him that. He was five and would be starting kindergarten in the fall. She wasn't ready. Maybe because it pointed out the fact that he wouldn't always need her. He'd go off to college and meet some scary girl who would take him away for good.

She laughed softy at her own maudlin thoughts. She was twenty-four years old. She was two semesters away from finishing a degree in communications, and as soon as she was able to return home, she would fall back into her familiar, comfortable routine. She had her whole life ahead of her.

So why did she feel despondent?

The answer was simple. She wanted Trent to trust her. To ensure Allen's future, she had no choice but to insist on a paternity test. But everything inside her rebelled at that thought. She didn't want a litigious battle with the Sinclair family.

She wanted Mac, Trent, Gage and Sloan to admit that she was one of them, blood or not. She wanted an apology. She wanted to see more in Trent's face than suspicion and anger.

Her daddy used to say, "Men in prison want out." So what?

She was sitting on a bench, packages tucked beside her, when Trent returned. Without speaking, he got out, opened the trunk and waited for her to put her shopping spoils inside.

Then he faced her across the roof of the car, his expression stoic. "Where would you like to eat?"

Bryn's temper had a long fuse, but his manner was insulting. She glared at him. "There's a sandwich shop on the corner. We can grab something and eat on the way home…so we don't waste any time."

Her sarcasm hit the mark. He opened his

mouth and shut it again, displeasure marking his patrician features. "Fine."

Twenty minutes later, they were on the road. Bryn chewed a turkey sandwich that felt like sand in her mouth. Finally, she gave up and wrapped most of it in the waxed paper and stuffed it in the bag.

Trent had finished his without fanfare and was sipping coffee and staring out the windshield in the dwindling light. Encountering large wildlife on the road was always a hazard, but Trent was a careful driver and Bryn felt perfectly safe with him.

She chewed her lip, wishing she could go back in time and erase every stupid thing she'd ever done. Including the day she invited Trent to take her to the prom. Trent had said no, of course. Bryn had cried her eyes out behind the barn, and Jesse had come along to comfort her.

In retrospect, she suspected Jesse's motive, even from that first moment, had been troublemaking.

When the silence in the car became unbearably oppressive, Bryn put her hand on Trent's sleeve. "I'm really sorry about Jesse. I know you loved him very much." She felt the muscles in his forearm tense, so she took her hand away. Apparently even brief contact with her disgusted him.

Trent drummed his fingers on the steering wheel, his profile bleak. "I still can't believe it. He was such a good kid."

"You weren't around him much in the last several years, though. He changed a lot."

"What do you mean?" The words were sharp.

"Didn't you wonder why he never graduated from college?"

"Dad said he had trouble settling on a major. He was restless and confused. So he switched schools several times. Apparently he decided he wanted to get more involved with the ranch."

Bryn groaned inwardly. It was worse than she thought. Mac clearly must have known about

Jesse's problems, but apparently he had done a bang-up job of keeping that information from his other three sons.

Did Bryn have the right to dispel the myths?

She thought of little Allen, and the answer was clear.

"Trent—" she sighed "—Jesse got kicked out of four universities for excessive drinking and drug use. Your father finally made him come home to keep an eye on him."

The car swerved, the brakes screeched and Bryn's seat belt cut into her chest as Trent slammed the car to a halt at the side of the road. He punched on the overhead light and turned to face her. "How dare you try to smear my brother's memory.… You have no right." His dark eyes flashed, and the curve of his sensual lips was tight.

She wouldn't back down, not now. "I'm sorry," she said softly. "I really am. But Mac has done you a disservice. Perhaps you could have helped if you had known."

Trent's laser gaze would have ripped her in half if she hadn't known in her heart she was doing the right thing. Pain etched his face, along with confusion and remorse, and a seldom-seen, heart-wrenching vulnerability—at least not by Bryn.

He ran a hand through his hair. "You're lying again. How would you know anything about Jesse?"

Denial was a normal stage of grief. But Bryn held firm. "I'm not lying," she said calmly. "Jesse called me a couple or three times a year. And every time it was the same. He was either drunk or high. He'd ramble on about how he wanted me to come back to Wyoming."

"If you're telling the truth, it's even worse. He might have wanted to make a family with you and the baby, even if it wasn't his."

"Focus, Trent. He didn't know what he was saying half the time. If anything, he wanted to use me and Allen to win points with Mac…to help cover his ass after whatever new trouble he'd gotten himself into."

"Jesse loved children."

"Jesse offered me money to get an abortion," she said flatly. "He said he had big plans for his life and they didn't include a baby...or me for that matter. That's why I ran into Mac's study that day so upset. I thought Mac would talk some sense into him."

Trent's face was white. He didn't say a word.

"But instead," she said, grimacing at the quiver she heard in her own voice, "Mac put me on a plane to Minnesota."

Please, please, please believe me.

He shrugged. "With your talent for drama, you might have a career on the silver screen."

His flippant words hurt, but they were no more than she expected. He'd been fed a pack of lies, all right. But not by Bryn.

She sighed. "Ask Mac," she begged. "Make him tell you the truth."

Trent shook his head slowly. "My father nearly

died. He's grieving over the loss of his son. No way in hell am I going to upset him with your wild accusations."

She slumped back in her seat and turned her head so he wouldn't see her cry. "Well, then— we're at an impasse. Take me home. I want to see how Mac is doing."

She didn't know what she expected from Trent. But he gave her nothing. Nothing at all. His face closed up. He started the engine.

Three

Trent was appalled by the picture Bryn painted of Jesse. The young brother Trent remembered was fun-loving, maybe a little immature for his age, but not amoral, not unprincipled.

Bryn had unwittingly touched on Trent's own personal guilt. He hadn't been much of a big brother in recent years. Other than Mac's birthday in the fall, and Thanksgiving and Christmas, Trent had seldom made the trip home from Colorado to Wyoming.

His company was wildly successful, and

the atmosphere of cutthroat competition was consuming and addictive. He'd made obscene amounts of money in a very short time period, but it was the challenge that kept him going. He thrived on being the best.

But at what cost? Had he missed the signs that Jesse was struggling? Or had the truth been kept from him deliberately? Gage wouldn't have known. He was usually halfway around the word on any given day. And Sloan was more attuned to the world of numbers and formulas than emotions and personalities. No…Trent should have been the one to see it, and he'd been too damned busy to help.

Of course, there was always the possibility that Bryn was exaggerating…or even inventing the entire scenario. That was the most palatable choice. But though he was far from being willing to trust her, the passionate sincerity in her eyes and in her words would be difficult to fabricate.

When they pulled up in front of the house,

Bryn got out and retrieved her packages before he could help her. Her body language wasn't difficult to read. She was angry.

He took her arm before she walked away, registering the slender bones. "I don't want you talking to Mac about Jesse. Not for a while. God knows what you're hoping to get out of this sudden, compassionate visit, but I'll be watching you, so don't do anything to upset Mac or you'll have me to deal with."

She threw him a mocking smile as she walked toward the porch. "I love Mac. And your threats don't scare me. I think your original idea was the best.... I plan to stay out of your way."

Bryn saw little of Trent for three days, which was a good thing. She was still smarting from their most recent confrontation. He showed up in his dad's room several times a day to chat with him, and on those occasions, Bryn slipped away to give the men privacy.

Mac was aware of Trent's burdens and

complained to Bryn. "Can't you slow him down? The boy works round the clock. If he's not on the ranch, he's holding conference calls with his staff and staying up half the night doing God knows what."

"How am I supposed to stop him? Your sons would do anything for you, Mac, but it must be terribly difficult for a man like Trent to put his life on hold for a month." Trent had built a highly successful company from the ground up, and his drive and intelligence had enabled him to amass his first million before he was twenty-five. Even without the financial largesse he would one day inherit from his father, Trent was a wealthy man.

Mac frowned stubbornly. "He would listen to you, Brynnie."

"I don't think so. You know he doesn't trust me. He's got lawyers flying in by helicopter almost every day with contracts to sign. He's an important, high-profile businessman. He and I might have been close at one time, but I don't even know him anymore." The older boy she remembered—the young man who had seemed like the most wonderful person in the world to her—was long gone. The Trent of today operated in an arena that was sophisticated, intimidating and completely foreign to her.

The change in the man she had once been so close to made her sad.

Bryn wouldn't have minded the distraction of helping out around the house, but with Mac's revolving staff of cooks and housekeepers, she might as well have been staying in a four-star hotel. Any dirty laundry disappeared as if by magic, and her luxurious bathroom and bedroom were kept spotless.

For someone accustomed to caring for a child, working part-time and keeping up with school, she found herself at loose ends when Mac was resting.

On the third night after the uneasy trip to

Jackson Hole, Trent encountered her in the kitchen chatting with the cook.

His expression was brooding. "I thought I might see if Mac is up to having dinner at the table tonight. What do you think?"

She nodded slowly, wishing she didn't feel so awkward around Trent. "It's a great idea. It would do him good to get out of that room for a change." It was really more of a suite than a single room, but even the most luxurious surroundings could seem like a prison.

When the two men reappeared, Mac leaning on his son's arm, Bryn was helping set everything on the table. The menu, by doctor's orders, included as many heart healthy ingredients as possible, and the aroma was enough to tempt even the most uninspired appetite.

Mac picked at his food to start with, but finally dug in. Bryn watched, pleased, as he cleared his plate.

The conversation was stilted. But Bryn did her

best. "So tomorrow's the doctor's appointment, right?"

Mac had his mouth full, so Trent answered. "Yes. At 11:00 a.m. I'll take Dad. You can stay here and have some time off the clock."

She frowned. He made it sound as if she were the hired help. "But I would be happy to go."

Trent shook his head, his calm demeanor hiding whatever he might be feeling. "No need."

And that was it. The oracle had spoken.

After dinner Mac and Trent played chess on a jade-and-onyx board that Gage had brought back from one of his trips to Asia. Bryn could tell by the quality of the workmanship that the set was expensive. And she wondered wryly what it must be like to never once have to worry about money.

She stood unnoticed in the doorway for several minutes, just watching the interplay between the two men. The Sinclair males had never been the type to wear their hearts on their sleeves, but Bryn knew they loved each other deeply. They were a tightly knit clan.

Unfortunately, she was still outside the circle.

The following morning, Bryn was shooed out of the sickroom so Trent could help his father get dressed and leave. Unbidden, her feet carried her upstairs to Jesse's room. It was as far from Mac's as it was possible to be in the rambling house. On purpose? Perhaps. Jesse would have wanted to avoid his father's watchful eye.

A thin layer of dust coated everything. Mac paid a weekly cleaning service to come in, but they must have been given instructions not to enter this room. Nothing had been touched since the day Jesse died. Even the bed was still unmade.

Though it made her stomach hurt, the first thing she did was to gather a few items that could be used for testing…a comb that held stray hairs, a toothbrush, a razor. She couldn't afford to be squeamish. This was why she had come.

Bryn continued to straighten the mess as her mind whirled with unanswered questions. She had seen the coroner's report. Mac had laid it out in full view on the dresser in his bedroom. She suspected he wanted her to read it for herself so he wouldn't have to say the awful words out loud: *My son was a drug addict.*

What a waste of a young life. She picked up a neon blue iPod, plugged it into the dock, and flipped through the selections. Nostalgia and grief hit hard as she saw one familiar title, "Jessie's Girl." How many times had the two of them played that oldie at full volume, singing along, careening down a Wyoming road?

She had believed it with her whole heart. She had been Jesse's girl, and even though he wasn't Trent, he had made her feel special and wanted. She'd been happy mostly, relieved to know that she would forever be a part of the Sinclair clan.

But it had all been an illusion.

She opened the closet door and reached to put the sports equipment on a top shelf. As she did, she dislodged an old shoe box held together with a rubber band. It fell at her feet. Something about it made a cold chill slither down her spine.

She sat down on the double bed and took off the lid. She'd been expecting drugs, maybe a gun. Certainly not what she found.

The box held letters, maybe two dozen in all. As she riffled through them, she saw that the earliest ones were dated the year Jesse turned sixteen. The return addresses were all the same…a single line that read *RRIF.* The postmarks were all Cheyenne.

Had no one at the house ever questioned Jesse about them, or were they spaced so far apart that no one took notice? Or had Mac known all along? The three older boys would have been in college when the first ones showed up in the mailbox.

Bryn opened one at random and began reading. Horrified, she went through them all. Her stomach clenched.

What kind of mother would poison the mind of her young son, a boy she had abandoned when he was six years old?

The damage was insidious. A child might have missed the venom behind the words. But what about Jesse? Had he been happy his mother contacted him? Happy enough to not to look beneath the surface? Or as a young adult, had he been able to see the subtext beneath the whining, manipulative words?

Jesse, you were always my favorite.

Jesse, Mac was a tyrant. I was so unhappy. He wouldn't let me take you.

Jesse, I miss you.

Jesse, Trent and Gage and Sloan never loved me the way they should.

Jesse, you have my brains. Brawn isn't everything.

Jesse, you deserve more.

Jesse...Jesse...Jesse...

Bryn couldn't imagine why Mac's wife would have been so cruel. To punish her ex-husband? To bring discord into the family? Why? *She* had left them, not the other way around.

The later letters were the most damning. Etta Sinclair talked about her many boyfriends. She hinted that she'd had affairs while she was married to Mac. And she intimated that Mac might not be Jesse's father.

Bryn's legs went weak, so much so that she might have fallen if she hadn't been sitting down. It wouldn't matter if Trent and Mac ever believed that Jesse was Allen's father. Jesse might not be a Sinclair at all, and if *he* wasn't, then his young son was not, either.

Bryn gathered the letters with shaking hands, tucked them back in the box and went downstairs to her room.

Would there be any point in letting Mac see them? Best to hide them. Until she could decide what to do with them. Surely he had long since become immune to his wife's defection.

The more she thought about the letters, the more confused she became. She had seen pictures of Etta, though they were few and far between. Trent, Gage and Sloan were all carbon copies of their dad—big, strong men with dark coloring.

Jesse was blond and slender, the spitting image of his mother. Was it simply a quirk of DNA, or was there any truth in those letters?

By the time the men returned in the late afternoon, Bryn had almost made herself ill. She excused herself after dinner and hid in her room. After a shower and a long phone call with Aunt Beverly, she curled up in bed and read for hours until she fell into a restless sleep.

Trent's immediate anxieties were eased considerably by the doctor's glowing report on Mac's recovery. The heart attack had been a serious one, but Mac's overall health and fitness had mitigated some of the long-term damage. Mac Sinclair was a tough old bird.

Which emboldened Trent on the way home to press gently for some answers. He kept his voice casual. "Was it really necessary to invite Bryn to come out here? She's bound to cause trouble. You know what she did six years ago. I doubt she's changed."

Mac wrapped his arms across his chest, gazing pensively through the windshield. "I handled things all wrong back then. She deserves a fair hearing. That's why I asked her to come."

Trent was stunned. "But she lied."

Mac shrugged. "Maybe she did, maybe she didn't. But it still does my heart good to see her again."

Trent opened his mouth to protest, but choked back the words with effort. His tough father had never been prone to sentimentality. Trent feared that in this vulnerable state his father might be fooled by a woman who was beautiful, charming and had a not-so-secret agenda.

He spoke carefully. "It would be human nature if Bryn wanted a piece of the pie." Trent's job, like it or not, would be to ferret out the truth and protect his father from doing anything rash.

"Bryn is not a threat," Mac insisted. "She's the same girl she always was."

"That's what worries me. I can't forget what she tried to do to Jesse." Trent, too, felt the pull of Bryn's charisma, acknowledged the presence of nostalgic memories and emotions. But he was not so easily swayed by soft smiles and sweet words. He'd been in business long enough to know that people were not always what they seemed.

"Jesse played a part in what happened six years ago."

"All I'm asking, Dad, is that you don't promise her anything. Bryn might look like a dark-headed angel, but that doesn't mean she isn't out to get what she wants by fair means or foul." Trent would be wise to remember his own advice the next time he had an urge to taste those lush lips.

Mac moved restlessly in his seat, clearly exhausted by the outing. "You're paranoid, boy. Don't be so suspicious."

"I'll try, Dad. For your sake." Trent lived by the adage "Keep your friends close and your enemies closer." Whether or not Bryn was an enemy remained to be seen, but in the meantime, he'd keep an eye on her. She wasn't the only one who could put on an act. He would pretend to be the gracious host, and if she let down her guard, he'd be able to circumvent any mischief she might have in mind.

Tension and stress threatened to turn Bryn into an insomniac. After one particularly restless night, there was a knock at her bedroom door, and she realized with chagrin that the sun was shining brightly through a crack in the draperies.

She cleared her throat. "Come in." She expected the cleaning lady. But it was Trent.

The grimace that crossed his handsome face might almost have been a lopsided half smile. "I owe you a thank-you for coming so quickly when Mac called."

She sat up in bed, covers clutched to her chest, and scraped the hair from her face. Trent was clean shaven and his hair was still damp from his shower. In contrast, Bryn was decidedly rumpled.

He'd brought scrambled eggs and toast. It was all arranged on a tray with coffee, jam and a napkin.

He set it on the dresser and kept his distance.

She tried to clear her sleep-fogged throat. "Thank you."

His brooding gaze studied her. "One of Mac's old college buddies is coming to visit today. I thought you and I should make ourselves scarce.

It's a beautiful day. We could take a hike…like we used to."

"A hike?" Her coffee-deprived brain was slow to catch up.

He nodded, still unsmiling. "We got off on the wrong foot this week, Bryn. I appreciate what you're doing for Mac."

"So this is an olive branch?" Her heart leaped in her chest.

He shrugged. "I wouldn't say that. But it bothers him when we're at each other's throats. We can at least put on a good front when we're around him. So maybe we need to clear the air."

The breakfast was delicious, but Bryn chewed and swallowed absently, still pondering Trent's final cryptic statement. He'd left her bedroom abruptly, and he didn't sound like a man who was suddenly convinced she was telling the truth. If anything, he wanted to brush the past under the rug.

She couldn't do that. She had Allen to consider.

She dressed rapidly in light hiking pants and a short-sleeved shirt. She hadn't brought her boots with her on the plane, because they were heavy, so a sturdy pair of sneakers would have to do.

Sunshine must be strong medicine, because she found Mac in good spirits. She smoothed his sheets absently. "Are you sure you'll be okay while we're gone?"

Mac nodded. "I'm fine. No need to hover. You've been in Minnesota a long time. Get out and enjoy the ranch."

Bryn and Trent left shortly thereafter, this time in one of the ranch Jeeps. Trent drove with the quiet confidence that was so characteristic of him.

Bryn wasn't entirely comfortable with his silence. "Where are we going?" she asked.

Trent shifted into low gear as they wound

partway up the side of a steep hill. "Falcon Ridge."

There was no inflection in his voice, but Bryn felt a kick of excitement. Falcon Ridge was a family favorite. She and Mac's boys had spent many a happy afternoon there over the years.

Trent parked the Jeep and got out. He attached the quilt like a bedroll at the base of his high-tech pack and stuffed their picnic lunch inside.

"I can carry something," Bryn said.

His motions were quick and methodical. "I've got it."

The trail was only a mile long, but it went up, up, up. Trent led the way, his stride steady, his back straight. Bryn's leg muscles were burning and her lungs gasping for air when they reached the summit.

"Oh, Trent...I'd forgotten how beautiful it is up here."

The valley of Jackson Hole lay before them, breathtaking, magnificent, tucked against the backdrop of the Grand Tetons. A lone eagle soared on thermal currents overhead. Her throat tightened, and she wondered how she had stayed away so long.

"It's my favorite spot on the ranch." For a moment she saw vulnerability in his face and she wondered if he ever regretted moving away.

Trent spread the quilt, and they sat in silence, enjoying the view. Bryn was extremely conscious of him at her side, so close she could feel his body heat. He had leaned back on his elbows, and his flat stomach drew her attention. He was lean and fit and utterly masculine.

She had loved him one way or another for most of her life. When her parents died, it was nineteen-year-old Trent, more than anyone else, who had been able to comfort her. She had cried on his shoulder for hours, and finally, she had believed him when he said the hurt would get better.

If Trent said it, it must be so.

She tried to bridge the gulf between them, wanting some kind of peace. "You taught me to ride a horse…to drive a car. I always wanted you to give me my first kiss. But instead, it was Jesse."

Trent's expression was bleak. "That was a long time ago. Things change."

She pulled her knees to her chest and wrapped her arms around them. She was not the same scared, devastated girl who left the ranch six years ago. She had borne a child, gone back to school, learned to deal with life's disappointments.

But here on this mountaintop, she could feel the pull of emotion. And that was a recipe for disaster.

"What did the doctor say about Mac yesterday?"

Trent sat up, his shoulder momentarily brushing hers. "He was pleased with his physical progress. But he pulled me aside and said he's concerned about Mac's mental condition.

There's no real reason Mac needs you or anyone to babysit him anymore. Mac seems to think he's more fragile than he really is. The doc says we need to coax him out of that damned bedroom and get him back to living."

She flipped an adventurous ant from the edge of the quilt. "They say that even for a normal heart-attack patient that can be hard. But on the heels of Jesse's death..." She trailed off. They both knew that Mac hadn't dealt with either the reality *or* the circumstances of Jesse's passing.

Finally, still without looking at her, Trent spoke. "I'm sorry I didn't take you to the prom."

She was surprised that he would bring it up after all this time. "I was a silly girl. You were a grown man. That was bound to end badly."

"Still," he said doggedly, "I could have handled it better."

What could she say to that?

At last he turned toward her. "I was attracted

to you, Bryn. And that scared the hell out of me."

"You're just saying that to make me feel better." She couldn't meet his probing gaze. "I was so embarrassed. I wanted to crawl in a hole and die. Literally." Thinking about that long-ago afternoon made her cringe.

He brushed the back of his hand across her cheek. "I'm serious, Bryn. When you started dating Jesse, I hated it."

At last she found the courage to look at him. His eyes were sober, his expression unguarded. His small grin was self-deprecating. "He was my own baby brother, and I wanted to punch him in the face."

Her breath hitched in her throat. "I didn't mean for it to happen that way. I never should have asked you to take me to the prom. But then Jesse found me crying behind the barn and he promised to take me to the dance. He made me feel better."

"Because I had made you feel like nothing."

A jerky nod was all she could manage.

"I've asked myself a million times if things could have turned out differently. If *I'd* taken you to the damn dance instead of Jesse. We might have ended up together."

She rested her forehead on her bent knees. "*I've* questioned a million times why he asked me to be his girlfriend. And in the end, I'm pretty sure it's because he knew I had a crush on *you*. And maybe he thought you had feelings for me. He wanted so badly to be like you and Gage and Sloan. He spent his whole life, I think, trying to measure up. But he was never big enough, tall enough, strong enough. He was always the scrawny baby brother, and he hated it."

"Did he hate *me?*" There was a world of pain in that question.

She reached out blindly and squeezed his hand. "Maybe. At times. But only because he loved you so much."

"Ah, hell, Bryn…" The choked emotion in

those three ragged words made her ache for him, but she knew without looking that Trent would be dry-eyed. Stoic. He'd been the eldest, and as such, Mac had trained him in the art of keeping emotion under lock and key.

She turned to face him. "No one's to blame for Jesse's death. No one but Jesse. We make our own road in this world, Trent. He had every blessing, every opportunity."

His jawline could have chiseled stone. "This might have been an isolated event."

"Possibly," she said, trying to keep all judgment out of her voice. "But knowing what I know of Jesse, probably not. He had a dark side, Trent. You never saw it, because you never looked for it. He was your brother and you loved him. I understand that, I do. But Mac protected him and covered for him, and I think that only made things worse."

"You make him seem like a monster."

"Not a monster. But a pathological liar and a user. I know that sounds harsh. But Mac has done you no favors by hiding the trouble. You and Gage and Sloan should have known."

Trent felt the breeze on his hot face. He wanted badly to believe her, but what she was telling him was tough to swallow. Bryn had a young child to support. And she'd had six years to work on a story that would tug at all their heartstrings and open Mac's checkbook.

If Mac hadn't summoned her, she would have found another way to reinstall herself at the Crooked S. He was sure of that.

Suddenly, he wished his two brothers hadn't left already. Between the three of them they would have been able to determine if Bryn was telling the truth or not.

He let himself look at her, really look at her. A man could lose himself in those eyes. She seemed utterly sincere, but given what he knew, how could he take what she said at face value?

God, he wanted her. And he despised himself for the weakness. She was like a bright, beautiful butterfly, dancing on the wind. But if he reached out and grabbed for what he wanted, would the beauty be smashed into powder in his hand? Would he destroy Bryn? Himself? Mac?

He put his hands on her shoulders and the world stood still. Her eyes were wide. Shallow breaths lifted her chest, drawing his attention to the gentle curve of her breasts.

He laid her back on the quilt...slowly, so slowly. Her gaze never left his. And she didn't protest.

A wave of lust and yearning and exultation swept over him. She was his. She had always been his. Everything in the past was over and done with. There was no Jesse. No death. No suspicion. Only this fragile moment in time.

He shifted over her, resting on his hip and one elbow, leaving a hand free to trace the curve of her cheek, the slender column of her neck, the delicate line of her collarbone.

When his fingers went to the first button on

her shirt, she didn't stop him. "Bryn." His voice was a hoarse croak in his own ears.

Finally, she moved. She linked her hands behind his neck and tugged. "Kiss me, Trent."

The invitation was unnecessary. Nothing short of an earthquake could have stopped him. His lips found hers, gentle, seeking. But when she responded, he lost his head.

He plundered the softness of her mouth, thrusting his tongue between her teeth desperately, shaking helplessly when she responded in kind. He was practically on top of her as he yanked her shirt from the waistband of her thin pants.

The skin of her flat belly was soft as silk. His hand moved upward, shoving aside her bra and cupping one bare breast. His head swam. His vision blurred. Her nipple peaked between his fingers, and when he tugged gently, Bryn cried out and arched closer.

Her response went to his head. He was so hard, he ached from head to toe. Ached for her. For Bryn. He hadn't been with a woman in several months...and hadn't really noticed the omission. But now he was on fire, out of control.

As she worked at his belt and found the zipper below, her slight clumsiness tormented him. He groaned aloud when her small fingers closed around his erection and squeezed lightly. *God.* He was in danger of coming in her hand.

What kind of man put sexual hunger ahead of loyalty to his family? What kind of man betrayed the memory of his brother? He panted, counting backward from a hundred, anything to grab a toehold of control. In that brief instant, his ardor chilled and his stomach pitched. Bryn was either a sensual witch or a self-serving liar. And all she had to do was smile at him and he was her slave.

He lurched to his feet, sweating. She stared at him, her cheeks flushed, a dawning misery on her face. With dignity, she straightened her clothes and buttoned her blouse.

She rose with more grace than he had managed and faced him across the rumpled quilt.

He saw the muscles in her throat work as she swallowed. "There's something you're not telling me, Trent. Something important. Something significant. I don't think you're the kind of man to be deliberately cruel. Why start something with me and then back away as if I'm about to infect you? For God's sake, Trent. What is it?"

He told her what he should have said from the beginning. The words felt like stones in his dry mouth. "On the day Mac put you on a plane to Minnesota, Jesse came to me and told me the truth. He said that you had been in his bedroom repeatedly...begging him to have sex with you to make me jealous. But he refused. He told me you probably slept with one of his friends until you were sure you were pregnant, and you planned all along to say it was Jesse's."

Bryn stared at him, frozen, her eyes blank

with shock. She wet her lips. "That doesn't even make sense," she whispered.

He gazed at her bleakly. "The damned thing is, Bryn, it worked. I wanted you so much, I was sick with it. And if you had left Jesse alone, you and I might have ended up together. But you made that impossible. And then you tried to make Jesse take responsibility for another guy's kid. You disgust me."

She swayed, and he reached forward instinctively to catch her.

But she backed away, the look in her eyes difficult to see. He felt a lick of regret, a jolt of shame. It was partly his fault. If he had stayed away from her when she arrived in Wyoming, they could have avoided this unpleasant encounter.

She backed up again, her hand over her mouth. Suddenly, his pulse raced. She was too close to the edge of the drop-off.

"Bryn!" He reached for her again, urgently.

He was almost too late. Her foot hit the loose scree at the edge of the steep hillside, her body bowed in a vain attempt to regain her balance, and she cried out as he grabbed for her.

Four

Trent cursed. In the bare seconds it had taken him to get to her, a dozen horrific scenarios filled his brain. But thank God she hadn't fallen. There would have been little to have stopped a precipitous descent—a small ledge here and there, a few low, scrubby bushes.

He held her tightly as sick relief flooded his chest. "You little fool. You could have killed yourself. What were you thinking?" He held her at arm's length. Her face was white and set. He was rigid, his stomach curling. "Are you okay?

Tell me, dammit." The words came out more harshly than he had intended. She flinched, and then her expression went from vulnerable to stoic.

"I'm fine," she said. "No problem. Let me go. Get out of my way."

He ground his teeth. "Don't be stupid. You're standing on loose gravel. I'll help you."

"No." A single word. Two small letters. But the vehemence behind it made him feel like dirt.

Unfortunately, this was not a situation where he was willing to put her pride first. He didn't waste time arguing. He scooped her into his arms and took a deep breath. She went nuts, shrieking and struggling until her flailing knee nearly unmanned him.

"Bryn." His raised voice was the same one he used to put the fear of God into his employees when necessary. "Be still, damn it. Unless you want to kill us both."

She went limp in his arms, and he stepped

backward carefully, keenly aware that one misstep on his part might send them hurtling down the mountain. When they were finally on firm, flat ground, he set her gently on her feet.

"C'mon," he said gruffly, grabbing up their belongings and stuffing them in his pack. "We're done here."

Bryn lifted her chin. "I'll find my own way back," she said. And she turned away and started down the mountain while he stood with his mouth open, watching, incredulous, as she did just that.

His temper boiled. He lunged after her, closing the distance in four long strides. He grabbed her arm, trying to keep a lid on his fury and losing the battle. "Don't be an idiot."

When she stopped dead, he had to pull up short to avoid knocking her over. He expected her eyes to be shooting sparks at him, but if she had been angry earlier, that emotion was long gone. Her eyes were dull. "Are you keeping count of those insults, Mr. Sinclair?" She jerked her elbow from his grasp and kept going.

They walked side by side, traversing the wide trail in silence. He noticed for the first time that she was limping slightly. No doubt the result of a blister from not having the proper footwear for the rough terrain. Stubborn woman. He ground to a halt and stopped her, as well, by the simple action of thrusting his body in front of hers. He put his hands on her shoulders, feeling her fragile bones. "You can't walk back to the house. It's almost five miles. You're not wearing hiking boots."

Her eyes were wet with unshed tears. "I don't care," she cried. "Leave me alone."

"I wish to God I could," he muttered. As they reached the Jeep, he reached in his pocket and extracted his handkerchief. "You've got some dirt on your face. Let's call a truce, Bryn. Please. For twenty minutes. That's how long it will take us to get home."

Bryn knew what it was like to have your heart

broken. But the blow-up that happened six years ago paled in comparison to the utter despair now flooding her chest. Jesse's lies had been worse than she thought. He had poisoned his brother's mind so thoroughly, Bryn had no hope of making Trent see the truth.

While he maneuvered the vehicle over the rough trails, she ignored him. They completed the journey back to the house in silence. Without speaking, Trent dropped her by the front door before heading around back to the garage.

Bryn tried to slip inside unnoticed, but Mac caught her sneaking down the hall past the kitchen. Julio had left, and Mac was fixing himself a cup of coffee.

His bushy eyebrows went up. "What in the hell happened to you, Brynnie? You look like something the cat dragged in."

Hearing the affectionate nickname stung her battered heart. She opened her mouth to explain, but was overtaken by a wave of grief.

"Trent thinks I seduced Jesse," she said on a hiccupping half sob. "He'll never forgive me."

And then she broke down. Her body was sore, her feet rubbed raw, her emotions shredded. When Mac enfolded her in his big arms, she put her head on his shoulder and sighed. She hadn't realized until this very moment what a hole there had been in her life without his wise counsel and unconditional love.

He held her in silence for a few minutes, and then they went to his study and sat side by side on the oversize leather sofa.

Mac studied her face. "Talk to me, girl. Are you okay?"

Bryn managed a smile. "I'm fine...really. All I need is a shower and some clean clothes."

Then she bit her lip. "We're going to have to settle some things, Mac. I don't want to be away from Allen much longer. You're recovering on schedule. I know the grief is tough, but physically you're doing well. With lots of rest and healthy food, you'll be back to your old ornery self in no time. But I can't be here with Trent. It's an impossible situation." And with Jesse's parentage now in question her quest to secure Allen's future might be a moot point.

Mac leaned back, his arms folded across his chest. "It's my house," he said gruffly. "I invite whom I please."

She shook her head in desperation. "You don't understand what he thinks of me, Mac."

"He's wrong."

Her heart caught in her chest. Did he really believe her? After all this time? She hardly dared to hope.

Mac's expression was bleak. "I suspected as soon as you left six years ago that I had made a mistake. But bringing you back to marry Jesse would only have made things worse. You deserved far better. And Jesse needed…well, who knows what Jesse needed. So many things…"

"Did you and Jesse ever discuss me?"

He shrugged. "Not directly. But I think

he knew I was suspicious of his take on the story."

"But you never put him on the spot and asked outright if he had lied?" That was what hurt so much.

The conversation had tired him. He was gray in the face suddenly and clearly exhausted.

Though it frustrated her, Bryn put her own feelings aside for the moment. She was here to help him, not make his life more upsetting. She took him by the hand. "Never mind," she said softly. "It can wait a few more days. Let's get you into bed for a nap."

He allowed her to lead him back to the bedroom, but he was still agitated. "You can't leave, Brynnie. Swear to me you'll stay."

She tucked him in and smoothed the covers. "We'll have to take it a day at a time, Mac. I can't promise more than that."

After settling Mac for his afternoon rest, Bryn retreated to her room. She had no desire to run into Trent. She was still aching from the knowledge that he believed she had seduced Jesse.

She spent part of the afternoon on the phone with Beverly.

Her aunt picked up on the tone in her voice. "What's wrong?"

"Well, Mac seems to have softened. I think he believes Allen is his grandson, but I haven't had the heart to press the paternity issue yet. Mac's really frail, and Trent is either hostile or suspicious or both."

"You'd think that Trent would want the test to prove that you're lying and let his family off the hook."

"I think he's afraid I'll manipulate Mac's emotions and get him to change the will regardless."

"I didn't get the impression that Mac was so gullible."

"He's not, definitely not. But the heart attack has changed him."

"It will all work out, honey."

"I hope so. But there's more. I found some letters that seem to indicate Jesse might not be Mac's son."

Dinner that evening was painfully uncomfortable. Mac's animated conversation was so out of character that Trent kept shooting him disbelieving glances. Trent never looked at Bryn at all.

Mac cleared his plate and finally dropped the "pleasant host" act. He glared at Trent. "Bryn's talking about going home. And I'm guessing it's your fault."

Trent snorted. "If Bryn wants to go home, she knows where the door is. I'm not stopping her."

Bryn's temper flared. "Charming." Trent Sinclair was a stubborn, arrogant beast.

He lifted an eyebrow and gazed at her coldly. "You can't blame me for wanting to protect my father."

Mac bristled. "I'm not feeble, dammit. Do

you really think I'd let myself be manipulated by sentimentality?"

"It's not you I'm worried about." Trent scowled. "It's her."

Bryn felt her cheeks flush, especially because Mac watched the two of them with avid attention. In a flash, she was back on the mountaintop with Trent, his hand warm on her breast, his lips devouring hers. She cleared her throat. "I'm no threat to you or your father, Trent. And if you'd quit being an ass, you'd realize that." Her cutting reply might have been more impressive had her voice been less hoarse.

But remembering what had almost happened earlier that day made her knees weak with longing. The past and the present had melded for one brief, wonderful moment. But it hadn't lasted.

I wanted you so much, I was sick with it. The confession had been ripped from the depths of Trent's soul, and the self-disgust in his voice said more than words what he thought of her.

But fool that she was, despite Trent's obvious

antipathy, she wanted him still. It was only sex. That's all. Surely she didn't really crave a relationship with a man who thought so little of her.

She stood up blindly. "Excuse me. I have phone calls to make."

Late that evening, Trent sat at the computer in the study, brooding. He could no longer ignore the evidence before him. Jesse had been stealing from the ranch. From Mac.

The knowledge made nausea churn in Trent's belly. Why? Mac would have given Jesse anything he wanted. The old man loved his youngest son dearly. There had been no need to steal.

Cause of death: heroin overdose. The coroner's report wasn't fabricated. Jesse had taken drugs at least once. The little brother Trent remembered would never have done such a thing. But Bryn was right…Trent hadn't been around much in the last few years. Mostly because of a demanding career, but in part because the ranch reminded him too much of Bryn. And the fact that she had slept with his brother, or lied, or both.

He groaned and shut down the computer. If Bryn was telling the truth about Jesse's drug habit, then Trent had not known his brother at all. But if Bryn was lying, why did Jesse die of an overdose? Neither option was at all palatable.

Bryn thought Mac had protected Jesse by covering for him. Would Mac do that? Out of guilt perhaps…because Etta Sinclair had left her young son when Jesse was at such a vulnerable age?

Trent cursed beneath his breath and flung a paper clip across the room, wishing it was something that would shatter into a million pieces. He wanted answers, *needed* them. Was Mac strong enough for a showdown? Trent would never forgive himself if he caused his father to relapse.

He got to his feet and went down the hall,

treading quietly. His father's door was open, but the room was dim. Quiet snoring was the only sound. Mac slept like the dead on a good day, and now that he was medicated, he'd probably be out until morning.

Trent retreated carefully, only to find himself staring at Bryn's bedroom door. A light shone from underneath. It wasn't terribly late....

Five

She was shocked to see him. It was written all over her face.

"I need to talk to you." He shut the door behind him and moved into the room.

Her nightgown lay on the bed but she was still dressed. The lingerie was a silky swathe of cream lace and mauve satin. He swallowed, dragging his gaze away from it and focusing on her face. "I have to leave in the morning."

"So soon?"

"Not for good," he said swiftly. "But I have to

fly to Denver for a meeting that I can't handle over the phone. I'll be gone less than twenty-four hours."

Bryn nodded slowly. "I'll keep an eye on Mac. Despite what you think, Trent, I love him."

"Even though he sent you away?"

Her smile was wry. "I'm trying to let go of the past."

He prowled the small space between the door and the bed. "Some of us don't have that luxury."

She stood there staring at him with bare feet and a face washed clean of makeup. Young, vulnerable, sweetly sincere. "You can trust me, Trent. I swear."

His body hardened, and he groaned inwardly. How could he be sure of her when sex got in the way and clouded his judgment?

He shook his head to clear it. But when he looked at her again, she was more appealing to him than she had been mere moments before.

His feet took him to her side. Her pull was inescapable.

She stiffened when he wrapped her in his arms. "I'm not playing this game with you, Trent."

The quaver in her voice hurt something deep in his chest. "I can assure you," he said roughly. "This is no game."

He kissed her because it was the only thing he could do. Because if he didn't, something inside him would shrivel and die. Because he was apparently weaker than he thought.

She was everything he had ever wanted and didn't know he needed. Her lips tasted like toothpaste and something else far more exotic. His past and his present woven into one complicated package.

She fit him perfectly, her head tucked against his shoulder, her arms wrapped loosely around his waist. He slid a hand beneath her shirt and stroked the soft skin on her back.

When he tipped up her chin, their eyes met,

his searching, hers filled with an emotion he shied away from. He wouldn't let her twist him in knots. This violent attraction was about sex, nothing more.

Slowly, waiting for her to protest, to escape his embrace, he bent his head. Their lips met easily, in perfect sync.

He moved his mouth over hers gently, dragging out the pleasure, making his own heart race with the effort to hold back. What had happened on the mountain only whetted his appetite for more. This had nothing to do with Jesse. This was about scratching an itch. Or at the very least, proving to himself how far she was willing to go. He wanted her.

Clothes drifted away in a sensual ballet. Skin heated. Voices hoarsened with desire. His and hers.

This time Bryn was the one to call a halt. Pale but calm, she slipped from the bed and donned her robe.

"I want you, Trent. But not like this. Not with mistrust between us."

Before he could summon a response, the shrill shriek of the smoke alarm sounded. For one crazed split second, he actually thought about dragging her down on the bed and saying to hell with it.

But the memory of his father jarred him to reality.

He rolled from the bed, groaning and cursing, and shoved his legs into his jeans. "This isn't over," he said.

Bryn knew her blood pressure must be through the roof. To go from desperate arousal to anxiety to fear so quickly made nausea swim in her stomach.

She found Trent and Mac in the kitchen. Trent was swearing a blue streak, and Mac presided over a ruined skillet than contained the charred remains of what must have been eggs.

Trent climbed on a chair to disable the smoke

alarm. In the resultant silence, the three adults faced off in an uncomfortable triangle.

Bryn had the misfortune to giggle.

Trent glared and Mac chortled. Soon all three of them were laughing hysterically.

Trent was the first to regain control. "Good God, Dad. What in the hell were you doing? I thought you were sound asleep."

Mac's expression was sheepish. "I was hungry. And nobody will let me eat anything decent. So I was making an omelet...with whole eggs... and butter." He puffed out his chest and tried to face them down with bluster.

"I would have helped you," Bryn said mildly. She took the pan to the sink. "And since when do you know how to cook?"

"Since never. Hence the fire." Trent dropped into a chair.

Mac raked at the tufts of white hair standing in disarray all over his head. "It wasn't actually a fire," Mac muttered, sulking. "I went to the bathroom for just a second, and when I came back…"

"That one's a goner." Bryn gave up and tossed the ruined cookware in the trash bin.

Trent rubbed his forehead, where almost certainly a killer headache was attacking him. He'd not had the best half hour. Bryn felt his pain.

He looked up at both of them. "God knows I don't want to leave you two here alone, but please promise me you'll behave until I get back."

Bryn hugged Mac. "We'll be fine," she said, yawning suddenly. "Let's all get some sleep."

It didn't take a genius to figure out that any sexual overtures on Trent's part would not be repeated…at least not tonight.

There was an awkward moment in the hallway after Mac escaped to his quarters, but Bryn evaded Trent's gaze and slipped into her bedroom with a muttered good-night, closing the door behind her with a sigh of relief. Perhaps it was for the best. She didn't understand Trent's motives. And until she did, self-preservation was the order of the day.

Perhaps understandably, she overslept. She awakened to the sound of a car engine fading into the distance. Already it was clear to her that things were not the same. The house seemed empty with Trent gone. He'd always been a force to reckon with, and the world was oddly flat in his absence.

Instead of moping and trying to analyze the situation, she forced herself to get up and face the day. When Mac appeared in the kitchen, he was chipper and energetic in contrast to her aching head and troubled thoughts.

He ate his egg-white omelet and plain toast without complaint. As Bryn picked at her oatmeal, he cocked his head. "I told Trent this morning to leave you alone so you would stay."

She felt her cheeks heat. Surely…

Mac went on. "I let him know that if he didn't

have anything nice to say to you, he should keep his damn mouth shut."

Her pulse slowed to its normal pace, and she could breathe again. Mac didn't know about last night. How could he?

She twirled her spoon in the bowl. "I can handle Trent. Don't you worry. But we need to talk, Mac."

His bushy eyebrows went up. "Sounds ominous."

"Do you think Jesse's problems had anything to do with his mother's desertion?"

Mac's gaze shifted away from hers. His hands clenched. "Don't know what you mean."

"He was at a vulnerable age when she left. Sometimes kids blame themselves in situations like that."

Mac's complexion reddened alarmingly. "That was a long time ago. Jesse was a wild kid. Can't blame that on a woman who's been gone for almost twenty years."

"But what if she tried to contact him?" Did

Mac know about the letters? Was that why he was getting upset?

"Forget his mother," Mac shouted. "I don't want to talk about her...ever."

The change was so dramatic, Bryn was blindsided. One minute Mac was the picture of health. And now...

He shoved back from the table and stood up so rapidly he knocked over his chair.

Bryn reached for him in alarm. "I'm sorry, Mac," she said urgently. "We'll drop it. I never should have said anything."

He backed toward the hallway. "Jesse's gone. Nothing's going to bring him back. End of story."

Mac's knees gave out beneath him. His eyes met hers, imploring, scared.

"Calm down, Mac. Everything's okay. Really." What had she done? But nothing was okay, not by a long shot.

Six

In that terrifying moment Bryn was desperately grateful that Sinclair wealth meant having access to a helicopter. A 911 call ensured that medical staff at the hospital would be waiting and ready.

Getting in touch with Trent was trickier, and she felt terrible that she was disrupting his important meeting, but she had no choice. She drove herself to the hospital and waited.

Mac was still in emergency when an ashen-faced Trent arrived. "What the hell happened?

He was fine earlier. He drank his coffee while I had breakfast, and he was his old self."

Her eyes burned with tears. "I asked about Jesse's mother, and Mac went berserk."

Trent paled. "Dear God. Mac never speaks of her. Surely you knew that. You lived here for most of your life. Etta's defection wasn't exactly dinner-table conversation. Are you *trying* to kill my father? Dammit, Bryn. What were you thinking?"

The accusation in his eyes was made all the worse by the knowledge that he was right. She should have waited.

"I'm sorry," she said. "But I wanted to get to the truth. This family has too many secrets."

In Trent's gaze, she saw not one whit of the man who had held her so intimately only hours before. He'd come straight from his meeting, and he was wearing an expensive dark suit, perfectly tailored to fit his tall, virile frame. His shoes were Italian leather. The thin gold watch on his wrist could have paid for several semesters of her schooling.

On the ranch, she had allowed herself to think of him as a normal man. But now he wore his wealth and power with a careless confidence that only underscored the gap between them.

She watched as Trent paced the drab waiting room like a caged lion. Her legs wouldn't hold her up. She picked a hard plastic chair in a far corner, sat down and stared blindly at her trembling fingers linked in her lap. Last night she had touched Trent intimately with those same hands. It seemed like a fairy tale now.

The wait was agonizing. What if Mac died? What would happen to all of them? Trent would never forgive her, much less admit that Allen was entitled to part of the estate, if indeed he was. And poor Trent…to lose his brother and father so close together. *Please, God. Let Mac be okay.*

When a young doctor came out, Bryn leaped to her feet, but Trent got there first. She had the impression he might have jerked the poor man to him by the collar if it hadn't been socially unacceptable.

Trent's hands were fisted at his sides instead. "How is he? Was it another heart attack?"

The doctor shook his head. "He's going to be fine. It was an anxiety attack. When his pulse rate skyrocketed, it probably scared him, which merely exacerbated the situation. A frightening cycle, but not life-threatening. Do you know what precipitated this?"

Bryn took a deep breath, trembling uncontrollably. "I asked him a question about his wife. She left the family eighteen years ago. I never dreamed it would still be such a sensitive subject." She stopped, choked up. "Has he suffered any lasting damage?"

The doc shook his head. "No. I want to keep him overnight for observation, but that's merely a precaution. We did a number of tests, and everything looks great. He's a strong old boy, and I predict he'll be around to aggravate you both for a long time. The two of you can go in to visit him now. Room 312."

The doctor excused himself. Trent glared at Bryn. "You stay here. I can't take the chance that seeing you will set him off again."

"But the doctor said—"

"No." He was implacable.

She waited until he took the elevator and then followed him up on the next one. Hovering in the hall, she listened anxiously to hear Mac's voice. Thankfully, he sounded a thousand times better.

Trent's deep, resonant voice was so tender and loving, she almost burst into tears.

"How are you feeling, Dad."

"Embarrassed." Mac's querulous reply might have made her smile if she hadn't been so fatigued and overwrought.

Trent spoke again. "I'll stay with you tonight. The doctor says he'll release you in the morning. Apparently you passed all the tests with flying colors. Your ticker's healing beautifully."

"Aren't you going to ask me what caused all this?"

There was a bite in Trent's reply. "No need. I already know."

"Bryn told you?"

"Yes."

"Where is she?"

"I wouldn't let her come in."

"Oh, for God's sake, boy. Don't be a complete ass. This wasn't Bryn's fault."

"It sure as hell was. If that's the kind of loving care she has to offer, we might as well go back to hiring strangers out of the phone book."

"You know the doctor said I don't really need anyone to take care of me anymore."

"So send her home."

Mac snorted. "You'd like that, wouldn't you? You're gonna have to face facts, Trent. I'm ninety-nine percent sure Jesse lied to us."

Trent's voice was icy. "Then we need to get the kid out here, do a DNA test as soon as possible and find out once and for all."

A nurse, bustling to enter the room, jostled Bryn's shoulder and apologized swiftly. "I apologize, ma'am. I need to go in and take Mr. Sinclair's vitals."

Now Bryn would never know what Mac's reply might have been. The conversation at the bedside turned to medical details.

Bryn slipped away and pulled paper from her purse to jot a note to Trent. She passed it to the nurse's station. "Would you mind to give this to the visitor in 312 as he leaves? Thank you."

Outside, the fresh air was a welcome relief. She was appalled at her own lack of judgment when it came to Mac. Why couldn't she have left things alone?

She checked in to the small hotel around the corner from the hospital. Trent would know where she was. She'd left a note, after all. She wasn't running away.

With no luggage or toothbrush, settling into her standard issue room was a short process. After a long call home to talk to Beverly and

Allen, she eyed the beds. She was running on adrenaline and about five hours of sleep total. Wearing only her blouse and underwear, she climbed into the closest clean, soft bed and was comatose in seconds.

Trent prowled the hallway while an orderly gave Mac a sponge bath. The old man was at full speed already, bossing everyone around, and cranky as hell. But the episode had scared Trent badly.

He owed Bryn an apology. In his fear and upset, he had been harsher with her than she deserved. She had made a mistake. So what? It might have just as easily been Trent who blundered into a stressful conversation. He and his father butted heads often.

A nurse at the desk handed Trent a folded slip of paper. *I'm at the hotel. Bryn.* The doctor appeared at his side. "I'm going to give your father a light sedative so he'll rest this afternoon. Why don't you go get something to eat and come back around four? We'll call you if anything changes, but he's really doing very well, I promise."

Trent spent a few more minutes chatting with his father, but the medicine in the drip was already doing its job. When Mac's eyes fluttered shut, Trent exited the room and left the hospital.

In a small town like Jackson Hole, the long-timers all knew each other. The woman at the hotel desk was a classmate of Trent's. He gave her a tired smile. "Hey, Janine. Bryn checked in a little while ago, right? And she told you Dad's in the hospital?"

"She sure did. Poor thing looked beat. And you don't look so hot yourself."

He shrugged. "We're going to take turns sitting with him. If you'll give me another key to the room so I won't bother Bryn, and a take-out menu from anywhere—I'm not picky—I'll owe you."

He made his way down the hall and around

the corner to the room Janine had indicated and swiped the key in the lock. The curtains in the room were closed, and in the dim light, he could see a Bryn-shaped lump in one of the beds. His body tightened. He was determined to have her, even if she had lied. But it would be on his terms. He would be in control. With a low curse for his own conflicted emotions, he kicked off his shoes, collapsed on top of the covers in the opposite bed and closed his eyes.

Bryn awoke to the smell of pepperoni pizza. Her stomach growled.

Her eyes snapped open when Trent's unmistakable voice sounded from close at hand. "The doctor said we could come back at four. I left you a few slices."

She sat up, carefully keeping the sheet at a decorous height, and brushed the hair out of her eyes, deeply regretting the fact that her pants were three feet away on a chair. The covers on the adjacent bed were rumpled, indicating that Trent had napped, as well.

Less than twenty-four hours ago, she had been naked and panting in this man's arms. Now she could scarcely meet his gaze.

She licked her lips, faint with hunger. She had only picked at her breakfast before Mac collapsed. "Close your eyes."

"No."

His answer took her by surprise and she looked at him head-on. Dark smudges under his eyes said he was in no better shape than she was, but he no longer looked furious.

She frowned. "Then hand me my pants."

"No." A faint grin accompanied the negative.

She crossed her arms over her chest, in no mood for a confrontation. "A gentleman would have gotten his own room. You're rich enough to buy the whole hotel. So why are you here?"

He leaned forward, elbows on his knees. "Because this is where you are." He paused and winced. "I have a temper, Bryn. You know that. But what happened with Dad this morning wasn't your fault. You acted swiftly and responsibly. No one could ask for more. I'm sorry I yelled at you."

His unprompted and uncharacteristically humble apology should have made her feel relieved. But she didn't deserve his absolution. "It *was* my fault," she said doggedly. "I never should have mentioned Etta." She had wanted to find out if Mac was aware of the letters. And she was as much in the dark now as before.

"What made you want to talk about our dearly departed mother?"

The macabre humor made her frown. Did anyone really know if Etta was dead or alive? "Well…" She cast about for an explanation that didn't involve the damning letters. She would have to share their contents with Trent, but not yet. "It occurred to me that some of Jesse's troubles could have stemmed from her leaving you all at such young ages. But you and Gage and Sloan turned out okay."

His expression hardened. "We were older. We understood what she had done and why. We didn't weave any fairy tales about her coming back. At least not after the first few days."

"You were *eleven,* Trent. An age when a boy still needs his mother."

He shrugged. "We had Dad. And if Etta cared so little about her family that she could simply walk out, we didn't need her or want her."

Her heart bled for the stoic little child he had been. He wouldn't even refer to her as *Mother.* "And Jesse?"

"Jesse was different. He was only six. He cried every night for a month. We all took turns sleeping with him so that when he had nightmares, we'd be there to comfort him. He liked Gage the best. Gage would tell him stories about places all over the world…about the adventures the two of them would have one day. Jesse loved it."

"How long was it before he got over her leaving?"

"I don't know that he ever did. But he learned to man up and show he didn't need her to be happy."

But he did. Apparently Jesse had needed Etta a heck of a lot, and when he was a teenager, she wormed her way back into his life and drove him crazy. The thought gave her a shiver. She wanted so badly to unburden herself to Trent, to lean on his strength and counsel.

But with the specter that Jesse might not be a Sinclair, she didn't know what to do. It was naive to expect Trent to believe that Allen was Jesse's son without proof. She had wanted Trent to take her on faith, but *her* feelings were not as important as making sure Allen was taken care of.

Anything could happen to Bryn. And Aunt Beverly wouldn't always be around. Bryn had believed for six years that her son was a Sinclair, heir to a mighty empire that would make his life secure. The truth needed to come out. For all of them.

Once again, she eyed her distant jeans.

Trent stood, arms crossed over his chest, and grinned at her predicament.

"Aren't you being a little ridiculous, Brynnie? I've seen it all."

Her face flamed. "That was different."

"Different, how?"

"We were in the mood."

"I seem to always be in the mood around you."

His self-deprecating smile loosened the knot in her chest. A teasing Trent made her will-power evaporate. "We need to keep track of the time."

"We have all the time in the world."

He glanced at his watch, and her stomach flipped...hard.

He handed her the pizza box. "But never say I seduced you on an empty stomach."

"No seduction," she said primly as she gobbled

a slice of pizza with unladylike fervor. "We have to go see Mac."

His eyes were like a watchful hawk. "It's only two-thirty. I can do a lot in an hour and a half."

Every atom of oxygen in the room evaporated as their eyes met. Hunger snapped its bounds and prowled between them. She trembled as each second of the heated moments in her bedroom unfolded in her imagination in Technicolor images complete with scent and sound.

The crust she held fell with a loud thud into the box. Trent took the cardboard container from her numb fingers and tossed it in the trash can. He sat beside her on the bed and twirled a strand of her hair around his finger. "We'll figure this all out, Bryn."

The knowledge that she was lying by omission choked her. "I don't know that we can. Some things can't be fixed."

He kissed her softly, then with more force. "I'll make it all right. You'll see."

She let him hold her, but her heart ached. Trent Sinclair was a man used to winning, to conquering, to molding the world to his specifications. But even the king occasionally had to admit defeat.

He nuzzled her neck. "Don't think so much. Just feel, Bryn. Let it happen."

Their lips met tentatively. Last night everything had seemed new and different. Now she knew the truth. Trent Sinclair was a hard-ass as far as the world was concerned. He kept his feelings under wraps. But beneath that proud, arrogant exterior, he was a man of great passion.

She kissed his chin, his nose, his eyelids. "I feel guilty. We should be at the hospital."

"He's sleeping. The doc said so. Hush and let me love you." He stroked her back as he magically made her reservations disappear.

She heard the four letter word and managed not to react. It was something men said when they wanted a woman. He didn't mean he loved her. She realized that. She was far too intelligent to delude herself.

Which meant that she had to be smart about this. She wanted Trent. Badly. But now was not the time.

"You nearly convinced me," she said, her heart aching for a multitude of reasons. "But one of us has to be sane. I'll go sit with him. I'm sure you have some business calls you need to make."

Trent pondered what would have happened if they had not been interrupted last night. Today the mood was less mystical, more pragmatic. But she was as much a siren to him as she had been in the quiet intimacy of her bedroom. He reclined on his side, easing her down with him. Beneath her shirt, he traced the lace at the edge of her bra, feeling gooseflesh erupt everywhere his fingers passed.

Bryn studied him, big-eyed, her pupils dilated, her soft breathing ragged. Her chest rose and fell. She lay quiescent, passive. What was she thinking? He liked to believe he was a good judge of women, but Bryn was a conundrum wrapped in a puzzle. Young, but mature beyond her years. Inexperienced, but wildly passionate.

He reached for the tiny plastic hook at the middle that secured the two sides of the bra. As he unfastened it, her breasts fell free, lush, warm, soft as velvet. He pushed up her blouse and buried his face in them, inhaling the scent that was so evocatively Bryn. Her hands played with his hair, sending heat down his spine and making him wish they had all night instead of a snatched hour in an impersonal hotel room.

He would take her…soon. But he would delay his own satisfaction. This particular moment was about establishing control. He stroked her thighs, touched her center still hidden beneath satin and lace. Bryn groaned even at that light caress, her eyes now closed. He rubbed her gently, feeling her heat, the dampness that signaled her readiness for him. He increased the pressure, the tempo. Her hips lifted instinctively.

Slowly, wanting to give her every iota of pleasure, he slipped two fingers beneath the narrow strip of cloth between her legs, and then thrust inside her with a quick motion. Bryn gave a sharp, keening cry and moved against his hand, riding the waves of pleasure that caused her inner muscles to squeeze his fingers.

The eroticism of her release made him sweat. His erection throbbed with a burning ache. But he drew on his iron will and refused to allow himself to be at her mercy. Trent couldn't lie to himself any longer. He was soft when it came to Bryn. And it pissed him off that he didn't really want her to leave. His hunger for her was a weakness. And that vulnerability was trying to persuade him that she was innocent. That she was telling the truth.

Which made him the world's biggest jackass. Powerful men were brought down by scheming women all the time. He hoped like hell she

was being honest with him. But if worse came
to worst…if she had lied about Jesse…well…
Trent's loyalties were clear. Protecting Mac…
and protecting Jesse's memory.

But the effort to maintain the upper hand cost
him.

He looked down at her broodingly. "You're
right. One of us should be at the hospital. And I
need to deal with the mess in Denver. I shouldn't
have started this right now. I'm sorry."

Her flushed cheeks and tousled hair made her
even more beautiful than usual. He stroked her
cheek. "Say something."

Her smile was wry. "What's left to say? I can
wait until you trust me…but can *you?*"

Seven

Bryn's heart slugged hard in her chest. She had let herself fall in love with Trent Sinclair.

In the beginning she had fooled herself, thinking that all she wanted was for Trent to forgive her, to believe her and to show her the same gentle camaraderie and friendship they had once shared.

Later, she had told herself it wouldn't be hurting anyone if she dared to enjoy Trent's bed. After all, she'd been living like a nun. She deserved some pleasure.

But now…oh, God…now…

She had done the unforgivable. She had tumbled head over heels, gut-deep in love with a man who was as inaccessible to her as the moon. Trent didn't trust her. Might never trust her. And even if the truth eventually came to light, Bryn had a child. Jesse's son. A boy whose existence might drive a permanent wedge between Bryn and the man she had always loved.

Even if Trent finally accepted her at face value, the situation was hopeless. Even the least intuitive person could see that a happy ending was an oxymoron in this situation.

She turned her head to look at the man who had wreaked such havoc in her life. He was seated on the far side of the opposite bed with his back to her. His voice on the phone was different…sharper, more commanding. She could almost see the employee on the other end of the call scrambling to follow orders.

But Trent was not an ogre. He was disciplined. Fair.

He would hate the description, but he was a beautiful man inside and out. Completely masculine, tough, steady, honorable.

She couldn't fault him, really, for choosing to believe his brother instead of Bryn. Jesse was his flesh and blood. And Trent had spent a lot of years looking after Jesse, making sure he was happy.

Much like Bryn felt about her son. She would do anything for Allen. Including risking Trent's wrath to prove that Allen deserved to be recognized as a Sinclair.

But what she could *not* do was let this thing with Trent go any further. No matter how much she wanted to…no matter how wonderful it was to be in his arms, his life, his bed. Already, her heart was breaking. They had no future…none at all.

She dressed quietly and slipped from the room. Mac was just rousing as Bryn arrived. "You look good," she said. "Let me help you with that dinner tray."

"Hospital food tastes like crap."

Despite his grumbling about the bland food, Mac polished off a piece of baked fish, green beans and carrots. His protest was halfhearted and she knew the collapse had scared him.

Mac sipped tepid iced tea through a straw. "Where's Trent?"

"He was on the phone when I left. He'll be here soon."

"What's going on between you two?"

She winced inwardly, but managed not to react. "Nothing but the usual. He still isn't sure he can trust me."

"The boy's a fool."

"You were on the same page not so long ago," she reminded him gently. "Until Jesse died and you had to face the truth. Give Trent some slack. He's doing his best. Losing Jesse has shaken him. Especially since it came out of the blue."

Guilt washed over Mac's face. He poked at a carrot with his fork. "I didn't want the three boys to know how bad it was. I thought I could whip

Jesse into shape, keep a close eye on him. I'm responsible for his death as much as anyone."

Seeing the proud Mac Sinclair with tears streaking down his leatherlike cheeks was almost more than Bryn could bear. She moved the dinner tray and scooted onto the bed beside him, putting her arm around his shoulder. "Don't be a horse's hiney," she said softly. "You were a wonderful father to all four of your boys...and a dear grandfather to me."

"I sent you away." He rested his head against her chest, his eyes closed.

"You did what you thought was right."

"Can you ever forgive me?"

"Of course," she said simply. "Aunt Beverly was so good to me. And Allen adores her. I'm fine, Mac. No harm, no foul."

They sat there in silence, both of them lost in thought.

Finally, Mac gave a wheezing sigh and moved fretfully in the bed. Bryn stood up and smoothed the covers.

He folded his arms across his chest, wrestling with the IV. "Trent thinks we should get a test... as soon as possible. So there won't be any questions. But I don't want to."

The packet of letters in her room mocked her. Would a paternity test destroy her hope of securing her son's future? "Why not, Mac? We all need to know the truth."

"I trust you, Brynnie, my girl."

At that very moment, Trent walked in. If he had heard the end of their conversation, he gave no sign.

"You're looking better, Dad. Nothing like a visit from a beautiful woman to perk up a man."

Mac chuckled, but the bland glance Trent sent Bryn's way made her knees weak. It was hard enough to deal with a suspicious, angry Trent. How on earth was she supposed to find the strength to resist the charming, seductive version? One glance from those dark eyes and she was ready to drag him into the nearest broom closet.

She cleared her throat, forcing herself to look at Trent. "I'm going to stay with Mac tonight. The nurse said they can bring in a cot for me. Why don't you go back to the ranch to check on things and then come back in the morning to pick us up."

"I thought we were both going to stay at the hotel." A frown creased Trent's forehead.

"It was great to have a place to nap, but I'll be fine here. And Mac says he promised several of the men the weekend off. Isn't that right, Mac?"

"Yep. Brynnie will be here if I need anything, and they're predicting storms tonight. I'd feel better if you were at the ranch. Do you mind, son?"

"Sounds like I've been outvoted." Trent's lips quirked. "But, sure. If that's what you want, Dad."

Bryn and Trent sat with Mac until almost

eight o'clock that evening. Trent brought cafeteria food up for Bryn and him to eat. In some ways, it was almost like old times, the teasing, the laughter. They avoided any and all topics that might be upsetting to Mac.

But finally, it was time for Trent to leave. He touched Bryn's shoulder. "Walk me out to the car."

She did so reluctantly, unwilling to be alone with him but unable to think of a good excuse. They stopped off in the gift shop and Bryn bought a toothbrush and toothpaste. She tucked them in her purse with the sales slip and followed Trent outside. "Call my cell," she said, "and I'll let you know when the doctor says he can be dismissed."

Trent leaned a hip against the car. "Okay. I doubt you'll get any sleep tonight. Are you sure you don't want to keep the hotel room and let us take turns?"

She shook her head. "Mac will feel better about the ranch this way." A suddenly gust of wind sent her hair flying. The skies were darkening as storm clouds built. "You should go," she said. "So you won't have to drive in what's coming."

Trent smoothed her hair behind her ears, both of his hands cupping her cheeks. His gaze was troubled. "I want to believe in you," he muttered.

The husky words went straight to her heart. Was she imagining the caring and tenderness in his voice? She stepped away from him, gathering her courage, though all she wanted to do was rest in his arms. "But you can't," she said, the words barely audible.

He thrust his hands in his pockets. "You expect a lot."

She forced herself to say the words. "I can't be intimate with a man who despises me."

For a split second, he stood, poleaxed, before his face closed up and a mask of arrogance cloaked his inner emotions. "I don't despise you, Brynnie. That's the problem."

She shifted from one foot to the other, wincing as thunder rolled in the distance. "Perhaps in light of Mac's most recent incident, we need to concentrate all our focus on him."

Trent's black scowl sent a shiver down her spine.

She held out a hand. "Let's face it. We have nothing in common, Trent. You're leaving very soon…as soon as Gage gets here. Mac might get the wrong idea if he realizes we've been…"

"Screwing?"

His deliberate crudity hurt. "You were always special to me, Trent. And what we did this afternoon was—"

He grabbed her wrist. "If you say *fun,* so help me, God, I'll shake you, Bryn. But don't worry, sweetheart." A sneer curled his perfect lips. "I get the message. You have a short attention span when it comes to men. Maybe Jesse was right about you after all."

He lowered his mouth to hers, giving her no time to protest. But his lips were gentler than his mood, less combative, coaxing rather than demanding her submission. His tongue invaded her mouth, devastating, as he mimicked the sex act. Her knees went weak. She clung to his arms for support. Even now, with intense emotion radiating from his big frame, she felt no fear, no urge to run.

His hips were melded to hers, leaving no doubt about his state of mind. His erection pressed insistently against her lower abdomen. He was giving her what she craved…perhaps for the last time. And all she wanted to do was meet his raging hunger with her own desperate need for him.

It was over too soon. He shoved her away, his chest heaving. "We're not done with this, Bryn. Not by a long shot."

He got in the car, slammed the door and sped away, leaving her on the sidewalk.

Trent swore violently. How in the hell had she done it to him again?

Was she scared? Or was this part of a Machiavellian plan? Did she think she could turn him into a sex-starved, drooling idiot?

How dare she throw their lovemaking in his face? He'd begun to trust her, to believe in her. And she was deliberately trying to drive him away. He sent the car careening down the road, mile after mile, until reason prevailed and he eased his foot off the accelerator. He'd be no good to anyone dead. Mac was depending on him, and Trent didn't have the luxury of letting his temper reign.

Back at the ranch, he dealt with the various chores on autopilot, his brain racing madly to understand Bryn's behavior. The storm struck with a vengeance, drenching him as he ran from barn to stable to house. When he was finally done for the night, he showered and prowled the halls, wandering from room to room, the electricity in the air keeping him on edge.

He would have bet his entire fortune that Bryn's responses to him had been real...

heartfelt. Thinking about last night and this afternoon made him hard as a pike again, and he stood at the large plate-glass window, nude, watching the fury of the storm.

In his memory he saw the smooth perfection of her skin, the way her body responded to his touch. Her warmth. Her scent. His chest hurt, and he rubbed it absently. Jesse stood beside him in the night, a wraith, a painful puzzle.

"Why did you do it, Jesse?" He put his hand on the cold glass. "Why lie about Bryn? Why the stealing? The drugs?"

His only answer was the howl of the wind and the beating of his own heart.

"Hey, boss. Good to have you back."

Trent grinned at the young intern who had the temerity to poke his head into the private office. "Get to work, Chad. Or we'll cut your pay." The cheeky twenty-year-old from the University of Colorado was smart, self-motivated and had fought hard for this unpaid position. He reminded Trent a little of himself at that age.

When the door closed once again, Trent got up from his broad cherry desk and paced the expanse of thick royal-blue carpet. The huge plate-glass window on the opposite wall show-cased Denver's downtown skyline, but Trent barely spared it a glance.

After making sure Mac was safely back on his home turf, Trent had come to Denver again to wrap up the business that had been interrupted. He'd half expected the adrenaline of his usual routine to keep his mind off Bryn.

It hadn't worked.

He told himself that he was glad to be back in the office…that the rush of trying to pack two weeks of work into seventy-two hours was exhilarating. And to some extent it was. But for the first time in forever, his personal life took center stage, no matter how hard he tried to pretend otherwise.

His secretary, Carol, was the next to interrupt.

"Just wanted to remind you that Mr. Greenfield will be here in twenty minutes. Will you be using the conference room?"

"Yes. And please make sure Ed and Terrence are there."

She nodded and started to leave.

Trent held up a hand to stop her. "Carol…do you think I'm a good judge of character?"

She laughed and then realized he was serious. "I've never seen anyone put anything past you."

"Thanks." He was embarrassed suddenly.

"Is there a problem I can help with?" Her head tilted at a quizzical angle.

"No, not really. Just a situation with a woman."

Her eyebrows went up, and he felt himself go red. "Never mind. Forget I said anything."

The older woman grinned. "One piece of advice, if you don't mind. Don't ever assume you can use business principles in a personal interaction with the female sex. That will blow up every time."

When she closed the door quietly behind her, Trent scrubbed his hands over his face and groaned. He should have a plan before he went home, but he was damned if he could think about anything but getting Bryn in his bed.

He hadn't talked to her once since he left. On purpose. And Mac continued to evade questions about Jesse and the past. Trent felt like everyone was keeping secrets from him, but that was going to end. It was time for a showdown.

When business was tied up and Trent felt comfortable that his staff could handle things for another couple of weeks, he flew home.

It was late when he arrived at the ranch. He'd used a car service from the airport. His first stop was his father's bedroom. Mac was sleeping peacefully.

When Trent stopped at Bryn's door, he called himself all kinds of a fool. Before his knuckles could make contact with the wood, he jerked his hand back. He turned on his heel and headed for the barn, his forehead covered in a cold sweat. If something didn't break soon, he was going to go mad. He saddled one of the powerful stallions and led him outside. Only then did he see the silent figure perched on the corral railing. Had she been there all along?

He led the horse to where she sat. Before he could say anything, she beat him to the punch. Her features were shrouded in shadow. "It's dangerous to ride at night." Her voice was low, musical. He felt it caress him like a physical stroke down his spine.

He shrugged, putting one foot into the stirrup and sliding easily into the saddle. It creaked beneath his weight. "I *feel* dangerous," he said bluntly. "So you'd be smart to stay out of my way."

With him on horseback, they sat eye to eye. Heat shimmered in the air between them, despite the chilly Wyoming night. The emotions that had consumed him...anger...disbelief... disillusionment...all receded, leaving in their wake a sexual hunger so intense he had to grip the reins and clench his teeth to keep from letting her see.

Bryn held out her hand. "Take me with you."

Bryn was done with denying the inevitable. She wanted Trent. She *needed* him. She'd deal with the fallout later. His big body vibrated with something...anger...desire. He had every right to be furious with her. She'd run hot and cold like the worst kind of tease.

Was he still angry? Did she care? She ached with missing him.

For long, quivering seconds, he didn't move. Then with a noise that was part exasperation, part muffled laugh, he edged the animal closer to the rail and extended his arm. "Why not," he muttered, helping her sling a leg across the horse's back and settle between his arms.

She felt the warmth of his body against her

back and was excruciatingly aware that his big, hard thighs bracketed hers. Her bottom pressed intimately to the area where he was most male. She tried to scoot forward a few inches, but he dragged her back, letting her feel the imprint of his erection.

Her breath seemed caught in her chest, her lungs starved for air. All around them, mysterious night sounds broke the silence, but Bryn could hear little over the pounding of her own heart in her ears.

Trent held the reins easily, his body one with the horse. Bryn had ridden since she was four, but she had no illusions about her horsemanship. Without Trent, she would never dare attempt a night ride.

They started out slowly, picking their way out of the yard toward the road. It would be the only safe place for what Trent had in mind.

He bent his head. She felt his breath, warm and intimate, against her ear. "Forget about everything," he murmured. "Forget Jesse, my dad, your son. Let's outrun our demons while we can."

She nodded slowly. He was right. They both needed this. In the house, they were always tiptoeing, literally and metaphorically, Mac's welfare foremost in their minds.

Tonight, in the scented darkness, nothing existed but the two of them.

Trent urged the horse to a trot and then a gallop. The powerful animal complied eagerly, his hooves pounding the hard-packed earth, kicking up tiny clouds of dust. The speed should have frightened Bryn, but with Trent's arms around her, she felt invincible.

The horse ran for miles. The air grew colder as the night waned. Bryn's nose and fingers were chilled, but everywhere else she was toasty warm. Her head lolled against Trent's shoulder. She could swear she felt his lips on the side of her neck from time to time.

Finally, the horse tired. They were miles from home when Trent reined the stallion in and lifted Bryn to set her on the ground. Moments later, he joined her.

For a few seconds, she was confused, but then her eyes cut through the darkness. They had stumbled across a cabin far out on the property. The ranch hands used it mostly in the summers, either for work or when they wanted to cut loose and have some fun.

Had this been Trent's destination all along? Or had he come here subconsciously?

She swallowed hard. Trent was right. Danger cloaked them, locked them in a vacuum that allowed nothing in, nothing out. Her heart beat in her throat like a frightened bird's. She wanted him. Even if it led to heartbreak later. Tonight was all that mattered.

A narrow stream, much of the year nonexistent, flowed beside the cabin. Trent tied the animal with access to grass and water, and then turned to face Bryn. He was little more than a phantom in the dark night. Only his white shirt glowed. When he held out his hand, she stepped forward to take it. Their fingers linked…comfortably, naturally.

Once inside, Bryn waited impatiently as Trent lit a kerosene lantern and began building a fire. He squatted in front of the fireplace, his broad shoulders stretching the seams of his starched cotton button-down. His jeans were ancient, but the shirt was one of a dozen just like it. The Trent uniform, as she liked to think of it.

The combination of ragged jeans and pristine dress shirt summed up the mystery that was Trent Sinclair. He could go from polished businessman to rugged rancher in the blink of an eye. And both personas exuded confidence and sexuality.

Bryn felt the first ribbons of warmth from the fire. The room was small. Trent had created a roaring blaze that soon knocked the chill off the unadorned space. Other than the wooden chair where Bryn perched, the only furnishings were the straw tick mattress and the iron bedstead.

Trent opened a metal chest—thankfully

mouseproof—and extracted a couple of old quilts, clean but worn. Bryn's pulse jerked. Trent spread one over the mattress and dropped the second one at the end of the bed.

He stared at her. "You can take off that jacket, Bryn. It's plenty warm in here."

Was there a dare in his voice? She removed the garment slowly, aware that Trent's narrow gaze tracked every movement.

She wore jeans like he did, though hers were newer, and a simple, long-sleeved tee. Because of the jacket, she'd decided to forgo a bra. Trent's hungry expression signaled his approval. Her nipples hardened. He made no pretense of looking away.

He stalked her then, and she hated herself for backing up against the door. She wasn't afraid of Trent Sinclair. But tell that to her ragged breath and trembling limbs.

When they stood toe-to-toe, Trent lifted a hand and touched her chin, just her chin. "Is this want you want? Sex with me?"

A brutally honest question. No euphemisms about *making love*. She inhaled sharply. "Do you believe me about Jesse?"

He stepped back, enough that she could breathe again. "I don't know. Not yet. It's too soon to tell."

Her head dropped. "I see."

He touched the soft fall of her hair. "I'm not sure that you do. He was my brother, Bryn. And I loved him. He died in suspicious circumstances, and I can't wrap my head around that."

"So what are you saying?"

He shrugged. "I don't know what the future will bring. I'm not convinced of your motives or your reasons for being here. But I can put that aside for the moment if you can."

"To have sex."

"Yes. We ache for each other. Don't pretend you don't know it. We've been waiting six years for this. That's a long time to want something. I need you."

I need you. The stark statement was a gift in its own way. The unflappable Trent Sinclair had allowed her a glimpse of his vulnerability. She could throw it in his face...try to hurt him. But any pain she inflicted would ricochet and shred her heart in the process.

She shoved her hands in her pockets, feeling as if she might fly apart. "And afterward?"

A flush of color marked his cheekbones, and his dark eyes glittered with desire. "I don't think once will be enough. I want to take you over and over and over until we're both too weak to stand."

She gasped and covered the sound with a cough. The image painted by his stark words made her tremble with yearning. He wanted her. He needed her. Could she bear it if he turned on her when the deed was done?

"I'm scared."

His wicked grin was a slash of white teeth. "You should be, Bryn. You definitely should be."

Eight

A violent crack of thunder made them both jump. Bryn's shaky laugh held nerves. "At least you're honest."

He sighed raggedly, wanting to make her happy, wanting to reassure her. "Nothing on earth could stop me from taking you in the next five minutes, Bryn," he said. "Unless you change your mind."

His outward calm was hard-won. He wanted to ravage her, rip the clothes from her body, and plunge inside her until the torment in his gut subsided.

"I won't." Her gaze was steady.

Suddenly he was consumed by a wave of tenderness. "Come here," he said, the simple words guttural and low.

She hesitated long enough to terrify him, and then she closed the small gap between them. She lifted her hands to his face, cupping his cheeks, staring into his eyes as if she could delve the secrets of his heart. "I'm here," she whispered. "I'm here."

He lifted her in his arms and carried her to their makeshift bed. He had imagined having sex with Bryn a million times over the years, but in his fantasies, there was always a luxurious bed, scented sheets, quiet music. Reality was a stark contrast, but he couldn't have stopped if he wanted to. His only regret was that Bryn might be disappointed.

He laid her down carefully and stood over her. "If you want to say no, now is the time." If she did, it would cripple him. But he was damned if he'd let her accuse him of forcing her.

She curled on her side, one hand tucked beneath her cheek. "I won't say no. But I'm not sure this is wise."

He groaned, ripping off his clothes and tossing them aside. "It isn't wise. It's insane, Bryn. But to hell with everything else. Surely we deserve this one night."

The bed creaked as he knelt and made short work of undressing her. Her skin was smooth, pure cream. Naked, she looked infinitely smaller and more fragile. Innocent. But she had the curves of a woman, and his hands shook as he touched her reverently.

Her breasts were sensitive, and he spent what seemed like hours kissing them, weighing their plump firmness in his palms, teasing the pert, dark pink nipples with his tongue and teeth. Each gasp and moan fed his hunger.

When he saw her bite her lip, he put the back of his hand to her hot cheek. "Don't be embarrassed. I love watching you respond to my touch. You're beautiful. Even more now than when you were eighteen."

"I have stretch marks." Her eyes shadowed with insecurities.

He stilled, not wanting the intrusion of the past to ruin the present. An unseen little boy came between them for a moment, and Trent's brain shied away from acknowledging the conflict that lingered just offstage.

With a shaky hand, he swallowed hard, forcing himself to trace one faint silvery line at her hip. "No mother should ever apologize for that. You are young and lovely and sexy as hell."

He wasn't sure if what he saw in her eyes was gratitude or doubt. "No regrets," he said huskily. "Tonight's all about pleasure."

The pupils in her eyes were dilated, her breathing rapid. "Then I want to touch you," she said. She pushed at his shoulders. "Lie on your back."

Bryn hadn't seen a naked man in six years... and in truth, Jesse had been more a boy than a man. So, the reality of Trent's tough, toned body was enough to make a woman swoon. His skin was a light golden-tan all over except for a paler strip at his hips.

She paused a moment to wonder jealously if he vacationed in the tropics at some wildly expensive private island with a string of girlfriends, but she doggedly pushed the thought away. He was here with *her* now.

He tucked his hands behind his head, leaving her free to explore at will. His chest was firm and lightly sculpted with muscle. A smattering of silky, dark hair emphasized his upper chest, slid between his rib cage, and arrowed all the way down to his… She gulped, feeling gauche and in way over her head. Trent was an experienced man with sophisticated tastes.

What did she know about pleasing him?

Hesitantly, she placed her hands on his shoulders. His skin was hot and smooth. His chest rose and fell once…sharply. He closed his eyes. She leaned over him awkwardly, kissing his eyelids, his nose, his full, sensual lips. She didn't linger at his mouth. Too much danger of him taking over and derailing her mission.

Even his ears fascinated her. She traced them with a fingertip and repeated the motion with her tongue. She was shocked when her simple caress made him groan and shake.

His sharp jawline bore the evidence of late-day stubble. She liked the rough texture, because it made him seem more human, less polished. With his eyes closed, he appeared docile, but she was not stupid. Trent Sinclair was powerful in every way. For him to allow her such intimate access was a concession that was only temporary.

She moved her splayed fingers lightly down his chest, pausing to rub her thumbs over his small, brown nipples. He flinched, but didn't open his eyes. His jaw could have been chiseled stone.

Her palms burned from the heat he radiated. She reached his hip bones and lost her courage.

Trent moaned and, still with his eyes closed, took one hand from behind his head and grasped her wrist. Gently, but inexorably, he placed her fingers on his erection. He was long and thick and fully aroused. She gripped his hard flesh and felt a rush of excitement fill the pit of her stomach.

Carefully, she stroked him. His flesh tightened and flexed in her grasp. He was hot as fire, hard as velvet-covered steel, and so amazingly alive. Without weighing the consequences, she bent her head and tasted him. His hips came off the bed, and he gasped.

His eyelids flew open. He looked at her with an expression that sent heat pulsating wildly between her thighs. He managed a tight smile. "That feels good, Bryn. So damned good."

The guttural words bolstered her confidence. She had no experience to guide her, but she wanted to know everything about Trent Sinclair.

What made him smile, what made him shiver, what made him shudder in passion.

She loved the intimacy of the act, the feeling of power, the exultation of being able to please him despite her naïveté. But he stopped her too soon, his expression rueful. "Not all the way. Not this time. I want to be inside you when I come."

Her face went scarlet. She could feel it. And for a moment, she panicked. Trent was a male in his prime, a dominant animal, a man set on a course with only one possible outcome. What was she doing? What was she thinking? Could she seriously spend one night in Trent Sinclair's arms and not pay the consequences?

His smile was more a grimace as he lifted her on top of him. "My turn. And this way I can see all of you."

The position made her feel horribly vulnerable. He had not joined their bodies. His erection brushed the folds of her damp sex and made her quiver helplessly.

He studied her body intently, his gaze drifting from her face to her breasts to the place where their bodies were so close to consummation. His hands gripped her hips. "You're beautiful, Bryn. But back then you were so young.…"

His voice trailed off, his expression troubled.

She was the one to take *his* hand this time. She placed it on her breast. "Nothing matters outside this room, remember? We're taking this night for us. Don't think about the past or the future. Touch me. I've never wanted anything more."

Her impassioned speech broke the spell that held him still. He toyed with her breasts, plucked at her taut nipples, tugged them until she cried out. His eyes flashed, and he came to life suddenly, dragging her down to crush her breasts against his chest as he kissed her wildly.

He thrust his tongue between her teeth, taking what he wanted. She tasted the wine he had drunk earlier in the evening, felt the urgency of his hunger as he explored the recesses of her mouth.

Her head swam dizzily. The acrid smoke from the lantern and from the fire mingled with the scent of aroused male. She smelled his familiar aftershave and the tang of his soap.

For a split second, as he put her beneath him, fear pierced her muddled senses. She should tell him...

"I want you, Bryn." His voice cracked as he nibbled her earlobe. "I can't wait." He reached blindly for his pants on the floor, found his wallet, and extracted three condom packets, still linked.

Her stomach clenched. "Are you always so prepared?" she asked petulantly.

"No. Actually, I'm not." His eyes locked on hers with determination. "But I've been carrying these around since the first day you arrived...for insurance. I knew how I felt about you. I've always known. And I wasn't going to let bad planning on my part put you at risk. Do you believe me?"

His eyes were warm. She saw the essence of the man he was in their depths. "Yes," she whispered. "I believe you."

She flinched involuntarily as he parted her thighs and she felt the tip of his erection enter her.

"Relax, sweetheart. I won't hurt you," he said gruffly. He stilled and kissed her eyelids.

But he did. It was inevitable. When he pushed forward, filling her steadily, he met resistance, tightness.

A half-dozen years of celibacy made her body unused to penetration. She gasped once, and then clenched her teeth. It was getting better already. The painful fullness was morphing into a stinging sensation that might be pleasure.

He reared back in shock, but didn't disengage their bodies. "Brynnie?" His incredulous gaze bore a hint of panic.

She squeezed her eyes shut, wanting to

concentrate on the incredible sensation of having him fill her completely. "It's okay," she panted. "Really. I can handle it."

But something changed. He continued to take her in deep, long thrusts, but he was so gentle, so protective, that her eyes stung with tears. He wouldn't say the words anytime soon, perhaps never, but his body was making love to hers.

His hips pressed her to the mattress, but he kept his considerable weight on his arms, looming over her in the flickering light. Sweat sheened his chest. He was breathing like a marathon runner, his eyes glazed with hunger. She whimpered as he ground his pelvis into hers, putting maximum pressure on the tiny bundle of nerves that controlled her release.

She wrapped her legs around his waist, needing to be closer still. This was what she wanted, what she had dreamed of for years. And the reality far surpassed her limited imagination. She hovered on the edge of climax.

She wouldn't have objected if he had

maintained the incredible sequence of penetration and release all night. It was that good.
But his body got the best of him. She felt his
sudden tension, heard his muffled shout, and
then groaned with him as he took his release
in a rapid-fire series of thrusts that toppled her
over the edge, as well, into a starburst of sensation that seemed to last forever. Trent Sinclair
was well worth the wait.

Trent felt remarkably similar to the time he'd
been half trampled by one of his father's prize
bulls. He could barely catch his breath and his
heartbeat wouldn't slow down, no matter how
much he tried to relax.

In contrast, Bryn slept in his arms like a limp,
weary, dark-haired temptress. He brushed a
strand of hair from her cheek and sighed. He
was in big trouble, because now that he'd had
her, there was no way in hell he'd be able to let
her walk away. She was his. That much he knew
with a visceral, inescapable certainty.

He looked down at their bodies. The way she clung to him was natural. Right. His arm tightened around her waist, and he wondered how long a gentleman would let her sleep before instigating round two.

He wasn't a completely terrible son. His cell phone was in his jeans pocket, so if Mac woke and needed anything, Trent was accessible. But the truth was, Trent and Bryn had the whole night to themselves, and some invisible, pivotal moment had occurred…though he wasn't quite sure what it all meant.

Bryn was almost a virgin…if there was such a thing. Her body hadn't accepted his willingly. She'd been fully aroused, no doubt about that. But he'd had a difficult time penetrating her incredibly tight passage.

Which must mean she had gone without sex for a very long time. And that picture sure as hell didn't jive with Jesse's description of Bryn as a seducer and a promiscuous teen.

He tucked the quilt around her bare shoulder,

lingering to smooth the faded fabric against her warm body. He was in deep now. He'd made such a big deal of trusting his brother because of blood ties, but more and more it was becoming apparent that Jesse was not what he seemed.

Jesse had stolen from the ranch, from Mac. And the money had been used to buy drugs... at least once. Though Trent fought the sickening knowledge with everything in his heart, it only made sense to admit that Jesse had funded a secret addiction via his access to the ranch accounts.

Jesse had described Bryn as a manipulative, sexually active girl. But the woman to whom Trent had just made love was innocent and inexperienced, her body barely able to accept his at first. So in all likelihood, Jesse had lied about that, as well.

For the first time, Trent allowed himself to think about Bryn's little boy. Somewhere in Minnesota there was a kid who might be a Sinclair. If Bryn was telling the truth, then Mac and Trent had treated Bryn abysmally. But what motive would Jesse have had for lying about his relationship with Bryn? Surely Jesse knew that Mac would have welcomed Bryn as a permanent member of the family.

Perhaps for Jesse the answer was painfully simple. Perhaps Jesse hadn't wanted the responsibility of a wife and child. Trent would never know for sure.

Too many questions. Too few answers.

He eased carefully from the bed and stoked the fire. It was 3:00 a.m. Soon he and Bryn would have to go back to the house. And then what would happen? Nothing was resolved. Was Trent going to confront his sick father with the evidence of Jesse's perfidy? Or should he clean up the mess and say nothing?

The trouble was, the Sinclairs had too many secrets already. Secrets that had caused pain and heartache. And Trent was no closer than ever to knowing how to sort it all out.

He slid back into bed, chilled, and groaned

his appreciation when Bryn's soft, warm body pressed up against his. Unfortunately for her, his cold skin wasn't nearly as welcoming.

She stirred and sat up. "Trent?"

His heart stopped. The firelight danced across her face, her shoulders, her full breasts...painting an impossibly lovely Madonna. Her dark hair fell in soft waves, framing her face. She was like a vision, a fantasy...

But when he touched her, his heart beat again. She was real. She was here. And he would take what he could, give what he could...as long as the night survived.

He was on his back looking up at her. All it took was a smile to make him hard. Her eyes were shadowed with exhaustion, her tousled hair a testament to their earlier lovemaking.

"I'm glad you came with me tonight." He couldn't resist stroking her leg.

"Me, too. I missed you while you were gone." She pulled her knees to her chest and laid her head on them, regarding him sleepily.

Despite the awkwardness of the question, he took a deep breath and made himself ask it anyway. "Why was it so difficult for you to..."

"Have sex with you?"

He grimaced. "Yeah."

"Why do you think?"

She was asking for something from him. But he felt as if he was traversing a minefield. "I don't think you've been with a man in a very long time. Is that right?"

Her lashes fell, and he could no longer judge her expression.

"I've had sex in my life a total of five times... all with Jesse. I had already decided to break it off when I found out I was pregnant." She sighed. "Since then...well, *you* try being an unwed mother, a full-time student and a grateful niece. Boyfriends were way down on my radar."

A sharp pain in his chest made it hard to breathe. She had been through a hell of a lot, and the responsibility for all of it lay firmly at his family's door. They had all let her down. Mac. Jesse. Trent.

He couldn't bear to think of it anymore. Not right now. Not with the epitome of every one of his fantasies just a hand's width away.

"Come here, Bryn. It will be better this time, I swear."

A smile flitted across her expressive face, but she allowed him to pull her beneath the covers. "It wasn't all that bad before," she teased gently.

She insisted on being the one to put on the condom. Her clumsiness was both amusing and arousing. He moved half on top of her, shuddering at the sense of homecoming. "I can do better."

He put his hand on her thigh, between her legs. She was wet already and warm, so warm. Being with Bryn was like basking in front of a fire on a rainy winter's night. She chased away the cold. And she filled him up in places he never knew were empty. Why was he so afraid to take her at face value? What more proof did he need?

She wasn't content to be passive. As he caressed her, she set about to drive him over the edge. She was a fast learner, and she was uncannily attuned to his body's responses. Her small, soft hands touched him everywhere. He burned. He ached. He struggled to breathe.

He heard her laugh once, and a shiver snaked its way down his spine. It was the sound of a woman discovering her power. And his weakness.

In the distance, the sound of rain drummed steadily on the tin roof. The seclusion lent a surreal note to the night's events. A wild, windswept ride, a deserted, ramshackle cabin. A man and a woman discovering each other's intimate secrets.

If he hadn't known better, he might have thought it was all a dream. He leaned on his elbow, winnowing his fingers through her hair.

His body insisted he seal the deal, but he was desperate to make the night stretch beyond its limits. He brushed a thumb across each of her eyelids, replacing urgency with tenderness. Passion slowed to a quiet burn.

"I wish we could go back and change the past," he muttered.

Her expression, even in the firelight, was bleak. "I have a child, Trent. I wouldn't change that if I could. Whether or not you can come to terms with Allen's existence will decide how all of this plays out. I won't hide my son and I won't apologize for him."

He was struck by her quiet confidence. She might be a novice in bed, but she was a mature woman with undeniable strength…an appealing mixture of vulnerability and determination.

Already her taste was like a drug he couldn't resist. He slid an arm beneath her neck, pulled her to him and kissed her. He shoved aside all the questions, the problems, the uncertainties.

One thing he knew for sure. Bryn Matthews was his. He'd worry later about the details.

Tonight was not the time.

Their tongues mated lazily. He was on his side with Bryn tucked to his chest. In this position, he could play with her breasts at will, could caress the inward slope of her waist, the seductive curve of her hip. One of her legs slid between his, and his heart punched in his rib cage.

The hunger blindsided him, not blunted at all by earlier release. "Bryn," he said hoarsely, "let me take you."

She spread her legs immediately. A rush of primordial exultation burned in his chest. He lost the ability to speak. Softer emotions were incinerated by his drive to find oblivion in her embrace.

He tried to remember her lack of experience, wanted to be careful with her, but his control had reached the breaking point. He thrust hard and deep, drawing groaning gasps from both of them. Her tight passage accepted him more easily this time, but still he saw her wince.

"I'm sorry." His voice was raw, his arms quivering as he tried to still the unstoppable pendulum.

She lifted her hips, driving him a half inch deeper. "Don't stop." She whispered it, pleading, demanding. "I want it all."

He snapped then, driving into her again and again, feeling the squeeze of her inner muscles as she climaxed, and still he couldn't stop. Over and over, blind, lost to reason or will.

The end, when it came, was terrifying in its power. He'd built a life on control…on dominance. But in those last cataclysmic seconds, his body shuddered and quaked in a release that was like razor blades of sensation flooding his body as he emptied himself into hers. It went on forever. He lost who he was. He forgot where he was.

All he could see through a haze of exhaustion was Bryn.

Bryn was everything.

Nine

They made it back to the ranch before day-break, but only barely. The storm had passed on, leaving only faint flashes of light in the distance. Bryn was boneless with exhaustion. Were it not for Trent's strong arms surrounding her, she might have fallen from the horse.

The return was no mad gallop. The horse was tired, as well, and they made the trip at a slow amble. Bryn wanted to cry with the knowledge that their stolen moment in time was over. Tomorrow, in the harsh light of day, all the problems would still exist. Mac's illness. Jesse's tragedy. Allen's paternity. The letters.

Just before they reached the barn, Bryn turned and buried her lips at Trent's throat. She felt his heart beating in time with hers. Awkwardly, she curled one arm around his waist, wanting to hold on, craving one last moment of believing that he cared about her.

Perhaps some of his hostility had been erased for good. But she was under no illusions. Trent hadn't said he believed her. Not yet.

He helped her down from the horse and held her close for several seconds before he bent his head and kissed her.

His voice was hoarse with fatigue. "Go get some sleep. I'll see you later this morning."

She knew he had to tend to the animal, but she felt rebuffed even so. Was that how it was going to be? Trent being his usual aloof, self-contained self, Bryn desperate for any scrap of affection he might offer. The picture that painted made her wince. She'd spent six years proving to herself that she was a strong woman who could put her life back in order. She couldn't let her feelings for Trent make her lose sight of the fact that she was first and foremost Allen's mother.

She had come here to secure her son's future. And to care for Mac. What happened tonight changed nothing.

Trent recognized the watershed moment in his life. As much as it hurt, he had to admit that Jesse was not what he seemed. Trent's baby brother had lied to, stolen from and hurt the one woman who had always been dear to the Sinclair family. The woman who above all deserved their support and protection. But Jesse wasn't the only villain. By their cruel actions, Trent and Mac were partly to blame.

Mac had begun the process of reconciliation. It was up to Trent to carry it through.

He decided on the front porch as neutral ground. When Mac headed off for his usual post-lunch nap, Trent lingered for a heart-to-heart with Bryn. She seemed oblivious to the gravity of the moment, and followed him outside without question.

Trent took her wrist. "Sit down for a minute. I want to talk to you."

She sank into a chair, her expression cautious.

"I realize that you were telling the truth all along about Jesse. Your son is Jesse's boy."

Her smile was watery. "Yes. Thank you for believing me."

He shrugged. "I still think we need to do some testing. For legal reasons. But Mac seems reluctant. Do you have any idea why?"

She shook her head. "I really don't know. He's admitted that he believes me, too. But I get the feeling there's something he's not telling me."

Trent took a deep breath. "Is there anything *you're* not telling me?"

Her unmistakable hesitation sent an arrow of astonishment to his gut followed by a painful shaft of disappointment. He knew her well enough to see the little flash of guilt…the way her gaze shifted from his. *Well, hell.*

The sense of betrayal he felt was crushing. He could persuade himself to believe her response was nothing important, but even his increasing desire for her couldn't make him ignore her telling reaction.

He clenched his jaw. "Bryn?"

She was pale, and her eyes implored him to understand. "There *is* something we need to talk about…but not in Mac's hearing."

"Well, that's convenient. When were you going to tell me this big secret?" Acid churned in his stomach.

She bit her lip. "It's not that simple. People can be hurt."

"People?"

"You. Mac. Your brothers."

His blood pressure spiked. His hands fisted. "Tell me. Now."

She held her ground, though she was trembling

all over. "I will. I swear. But now is not the time."

"Dammit, Bryn." He slammed a fist on the unforgiving wood of the railing.

"Your family destroyed my world," she cried. "And I've managed to forgive you all. But I won't let you boss me around. Your money has spoiled you, Trent Sinclair. It's turned you into an arrogant jerk. You think you can make everything and everyone dance to your tune. But you can't. Not me, anyway."

When she stood up, he took her arm, halting her progress. "Tell me."

She nodded slowly. "I will. Soon."

They maintained an unspoken truce throughout the afternoon and during the evening meal. Trent's frequent absences from the house made things a lot easier, though he did show up at the dinner table on time and carried his end of the conversation.

Bryn avoided looking at him, her attention

fixed on Mac. But she was hyperaware of Trent sitting only a few feet away. He was rumpled and weary, his jeans stained, his white dress shirt no longer crisp. But in a room of tuxedo-clad men, he would still command attention.

He was an alpha male, and he had the confidence of twenty men. She wondered bleakly what it must be like to always be so self-assured. She'd second-guessed herself a hundred times as a new mom, and even now, she often worried at night, when sleep came slowly, if she could give Allen everything he needed.

Not so much *things*. Between her and Aunt Beverly, they had a nice life of modest means. But sooner or later, Allen would need a father figure to guide him. Someone to toss a football with, to go on Scout outings, to learn what it meant to be a real man.

Mac might fill that role in part, if he were willing. But he was getting older, and his heart attack pointed out the reality that he would not always be around. Bryn couldn't bear to think of the Crooked S without him.

It was a relief when the two men left her to her own devices and headed off to the study. Bryn decided to make her evening phone call a little earlier than usual. She missed Allen fiercely, and she wanted to listen to his high-pitched voice telling her all the silly inconsequential things that made his day special.

In her bedroom, she shut the door, not wanting to be overheard. Her throat was tight, and if she got emotional talking to her son, she didn't need any witnesses.

Before she could dial the number, her phone rang, and the caller ID was Beverly's. Bryn smiled to herself. *Great minds think alike....*

"Hey, there," she said, her heart lifting. "What's up?"

Beverly's voice was solemn. "Don't freak out, my love. Little Allen is in the hospital."

Bryn's legs collapsed beneath her. She sat down hard on the bed. "What happened?"

"He's going to be okay. It was a severe asthma attack. I had to call an ambulance. He's stabilized, but he's crying for you."

Bryn had never felt so helpless. She swallowed hard. "Can you put him on the phone?"

"Of course."

There was a small silence, and then her son's weak, pitiful voice said, "Hi, Mommy."

"Hello, my sweet boy. I'm so sorry you're sick. Is the hospital taking good care of you?"

"I got ice cream for supper."

She closed her eyes. "That's nice."

"I miss you, Mommy."

The knife in her heart twisted. It was hard to speak. "I'm going to get on a plane, and I'll try to be there when you wake up. I promise."

"Okay." He sounded drowsy now.

Beverly came back on the line. "Don't panic, Bryn. He's perfectly fine. They'll probably release him in the morning. But I do think he needs you."

"I'll be there as soon as humanly possible."

* * *

Trent seated his father in the leather desk chair and pulled up a stool beside him. He put a hand on Mac's, feeling the slight tremor of his dad's fingers. Trent had gone back and forth about what to do, but the doctor had reassured him this morning that Mac was more than strong enough to face the truth about Jesse.

Trent pulled up the file he had saved on the computer and sighed deeply. "Dad, I don't know how to tell you this without just blurting it out. I've been working on the books every day during the last two weeks. I've combed through the accounts repeatedly. And I keep coming up with the same answer. Jesse was stealing from the ranch. From you."

Mac's expression didn't change. He turned his palm upward and squeezed Trent's hand. "I know, son. I know."

Trent gaped. "You knew?"

Mac took his hand away and leaned back in the chair, his gaze pensive. "I wanted him here so I could keep an eye on him. Offering him the so-called job of keeping the books straight was supposed to give him direction. But I track every column of those ledgers. I saw the first instance where he shifted funds—I knew what was happening from the beginning."

"And you couldn't confront him?"

"I was scared. He'd developed a terrible temper, exacerbated by the drugs, I'm sure. He was trapped in a downward spiral, but I couldn't seem to find a way to stop it. I was a helpless old fool."

"Why didn't you ask Gage and Sloan and me for help?"

Mac rubbed his eyes. "I didn't want you to think badly of him. You were his big brothers. He idolized all three of you. And I knew how much you loved him in return. If he had managed to get clean, he would have been so embarrassed that you knew, so I kept his secret."

"But Bryn knew."

Mac winced. "Apparently so. I didn't know it

at the time, but Jesse often called her when he went on one of his binges."

"She told me. And I called her a liar."

"Aw, hell, son. We didn't deserve that little girl. She hit the first crisis of her adult life, and we kicked her out."

Trent didn't protest being included in the *we*. He could have stood up for Bryn six years ago, but he hadn't. His jealousy and pride had blinded him to the truth of Jesse's poisonous lies.

"We really need to get a test done right away." Trent stood at the window staring into the dark night. "I think we both know that Bryn was telling the truth all along, but I want everything to be on the up-and-up."

"We'll tell her we believe her...that we're sorry we ever fell for Jesse's innocent act. And we'll redo my will to include the boy. But I think doing a test would be insulting to Bryn."

"She will probably welcome the idea."

Mac shrugged. "We'll see..."

"You'll want the boy to spend some time here."

"Of course. Maybe Bryn can stay over while Gage is here, bring the kid out, and she and Gage and I can show him the ropes."

A sour feeling settled in Trent's stomach. He didn't want his brother bonding with Bryn's little boy...or worse yet, Bryn.

Suddenly, the door to the hall flew open, and Bryn stood framed in the archway. Her dark eyes burned in a face that was ghostly pale. "I have to go." Her chest rose and fell with her rapid breathing. In one hand were the keys to her rental car, in the other, her purse.

Trent was at her side in one stride, gripping her shoulders. "What is it? Are you hurt?" He ran his hands down her arms, searching for clues to her near hysteria.

She put her head on his shoulder, her voice a pained whisper. "Allen's in the hospital. He's had a terrible asthma attack. He's asking for me. And I'm not there."

It was a mother's worst fear. Trent felt her anguish as if it were his own. His eyes met Mac's over Bryn's bent head, both men thinking the same thing. How many nights had they kept vigils at a young Jesse's bedside when he had struggled so pitifully to breathe?

Trent held her close, stroking her hair. "Don't panic. I'll take you. We'll use the next thirty minutes to pack and check plane schedules, and we'll be out of here."

Mac held up his hand. "Wait a minute. Let me order the jet, Bryn. You call the doctor and see if the boy's stable enough to fly. We'll bring Allen and your aunt out here and I'll hire the best private nurse money can buy to accompany them. It will give the kid something to be excited about and you'll enjoy showing him the ranch."

"I can't ask you to do that. It's too expensive." Bryn's face was tear-stained.

"I'm an old coot." He lumbered to his feet and laid a hand on her shoulder. "What am I going to do with all that money, anyway? Let me do this, Bryn. It won't make up for the past, but it would make me feel better. It's late now...they probably have him sleeping. In the morning your aunt can tell him he's going on an exciting journey."

"Would he be comfortable on the plane?" Bryn looked at Trent, her expression troubled, vulnerable.

"It's damned luxurious." Trent chuckled. "He can play video games if he feels like it. There's a bed where he can lie down. He'll be pampered, I promise."

She nodded slowly. "I'll have to call the doctor right away."

"Use my BlackBerry. You don't mind us listening in, do you?"

She frowned. "Of course not."

Trent carried on a conversation with Mac while Bryn was on the phone. "We can give the aunt and the nurse and the boy the suite of rooms at the end of the hall. They'll be close to Bryn, and she can keep an eye on her little one."

Mac gave him a narrow-eyed, knowing gaze. "Staking out your territory, are you?"

Trent didn't rise to the bait. "It's healthy for children to have their own rooms. Even I know that."

"Well, I'll tell you this, boy. If you have designs on Bryn, you'll have to move fast." Mac snorted. "She won't be here much longer."

Bryn finished her call. The doctor had given the go-ahead, so Mac got on the phone in turn and started barking orders. Trent did his part, as well, and soon all the pieces were in place. By 8:00 a.m. the plane would be staffed with a nurse and every medical convenience necessary to make sure Bryn's young son would receive top-notch care.

Trent went in search of Bryn. He found her huddled in a quilt on the front porch swing. The night air was crisp and the stars numbered in the millions. He sat down beside her and pulled her against his chest. "He'll be okay, Bryn. Try not to worry."

She shrugged. "It's what mothers do."

"Did you ever think about getting an abortion?"

She didn't answer for a long time, and he wondered if he had offended her. "I'm sorry. That was very personal."

She tucked the quilt more tightly around her neck. "No, it's okay. Honestly, I don't remember ever thinking of that as an option. I'd wanted for so long to be a real Sinclair. You five were the only family I knew. I had a hazy memory of meeting Aunt Beverly, but the ranch and you and Mac and your brothers were my real family, at least in my heart. So when I realized I was pregnant, my first emotion was joy."

"But that didn't last long, thanks to us."

"I knew Jesse and I were young, but we were in a better position than most kids our age. Finances wouldn't be an issue, and we had all of you to support us."

"So you intended to keep the baby all along."

"Yes. I assumed Jesse would be happy. But that was naive. He wanted to be with me because he thought *you* wanted me. A baby made everything too real. So he lied."

"And we believed him."

"Yes."

"What did your aunt do?"

"She was wonderful from the beginning. No questions, only her unconditional love and support. Which was amazing, because I was almost a stranger to her. She did want to sue Jesse for child support, but I convinced her not to."

"Was she financially comfortable?"

She put her head on his shoulder, her body limp. "No, not really. But I held out this faint hope that one day I'd be able to reconcile with all of you, and I was afraid if we sued for child support, you'd hate me."

"Ah, Bryn." He held her close, feeling sick to his stomach as he realized anew how badly the Sinclair clan had played their part in this scenario. She had believed herself to be one of them, and they had tossed her out on the proverbial street.

Bryn yawned hugely as he stroked her hair. He nuzzled her cheek. "You need some rest, Bryn. It's been a tumultuous forty-eight hours."

She yawned again. "I know."

The memory of all that had transpired between them hovered in the sudden awkward silence.

Bryn stumbled to her feet, nearly tripping on the quilt. He scooped her up in his arms, bedding and all.

"Trent..." she protested halfheartedly.

"Let me pamper you," he muttered, holding her close. "Relax. I've got you."

He carried her all the way to her bedroom and laid her gently on the bed. She was already in her nightgown, and her hair was clean and damp from her shower.

He smoothed her cheek with the back of his hand. "I want to stay with you tonight."

The only light in the room was a dim lamp on the bedside table. But he could see her expression clearly. "Trent, I don't think I can—"

He bent to kiss her. "I'm not talking about sex. Give me some credit. I only want to hold you, I swear."

She nodded. For a moment, shy pleasure replaced the worry in her eyes. She scooted over on the mattress, making room for him. He shed everything but his knit boxers and climbed in beside her. It would be hell not to make love to her, but she needed him tonight, and he was going to be here for her. He had a lot to atone for, and maybe this would be a start.

She nestled in his arms as if they had been lovers for years. The pain in his chest returned, and he rested his chin on her head, inhaling her scent and keenly aware of her soft body and silky skin. He cared for her. Bone deep. It had begun as an invisible tie between them as she grew up. And when she reached womanhood, he'd known deep in his psyche that he wanted her.

But he hadn't been smart enough to understand that some opportunities weren't always available. His ambition and drive to succeed had taken precedence. As an arrogant young buck out to conquer the world, frequent sex had been available and plentiful. Perhaps in the back of his mind he'd assumed Bryn would always be waiting.

It would never have occurred to him to try and win her from Jesse. He loved his little brother too much. But he'd been well acquainted with Jesse's attention span, and he knew, even then, that one day in the near future Bryn would be free. Jesse didn't have it in him to settle down with one girl.

But nothing had turned out like it should.

Bryn cared for him now, he knew that. Otherwise she never would have let him make love to her. But a mother's love and loyalty were fierce commodities, and she would stand by her son first and foremost.

Whether Trent had a shot at convincing her he would welcome Jesse's son was by no means a sure thing. And honestly, he had qualms about being a dad. His own father had lived by the "make 'em tough" model, but Trent doubted that was what Bryn wanted for her son.

And what if Trent had children of his own? Would he be able to love Jesse's son in the same way? He and his family had hurt Bryn in the past. It would be inexcusable to compound that mistake.

Bryn moved restlessly, turning in his arms to find his lips. She moved her mouth over his drowsily, murmuring her approval when he slid his tongue between her lips and deepened the kiss.

His shaft hardened, but the lust he felt was overlaid with a patina of contentment, seemingly an odd match-up, but true nevertheless.

He wanted her, but the need to protect her was stronger.

As she lay on her side, her breast nestled in his palm. He felt its weight and ached to undress her and caress her everywhere. She had become as necessary to him as breathing, and for once in his life, he didn't have a course mapped out. He didn't know if determination was going to be enough. No business model existed to tell him what a woman was thinking. No amount of money could buy her trust.

And there was still a secret between them... something she was hiding.

She fell asleep, her breathing slowing to a gentle rhythm. He reached for the lamp and plunged the room into darkness.

It was hours before he slept.

Ten

Bryn woke with a dull headache and a sensation that something was wrong. Then it all came flooding back. Her aunt's phone call. Her son's illness.

She scrambled out of bed and dressed haphazardly, pulling her hair into a messy knot on top of her head. It was almost nine. For God's sake, why had Trent let her sleep so long?

She made her way to the kitchen, dialing her cell phone as she walked. Mac was there, drinking coffee, looking old and tired. Corralling

Jesse would have been his main focus for many years, a drain on his time and energy. With Jesse gone, and once the grief dulled, surely Mac would regain his customary vigor.

She clicked her phone shut and paced. "Beverly's not answering her phone. What if something has happened?"

Mac reached for her hand as she passed his chair for the third time. "Relax, Brynnie. The plane is in the air. They'll be landing in a little under two hours. And all reports are good."

Bryn couldn't sit still. She went to the sink and stared blindly out the window. Allen was on the way...and Beverly. Now if only Gage and Sloan were here, she would have everyone she loved under one roof.

When she had herself under control, she sat at the table. The cook set a scrambled egg and some toast in front of her. Bryn was too excited to eat, but she forced herself to get it down. Mac passed her a section of the morning paper. One of the ranch hands' jobs was to make a run into town early every weekday to pick up the three papers Mac devoured without fail. It was an expensive habit given the gas consumption, but Mac refused to read newspapers online, though he was fairly computer savvy.

Bryn was too jittery to concentrate on the printed words for long. "When should we leave?"

Mac grinned. "Trent's going to bring the car around in thirty minutes or so. Think you can be ready?"

She punched him on the arm. "Very funny."

The trip to the airport lasted forever. Trent drove, of course, and he and Mac sat in the front seat talking ranch business. Trent had kissed her briefly when he appeared, but there hadn't been time for anything more personal or intimate. Bryn sat in the rear, her legs tucked beneath her, and leaned her head against the window, watching the world go by.

She loved Wyoming. And as much as she

missed her son and her aunt, she wouldn't have traded this time for anything. Being home— and it *was* home—had healed the dark places inside her. She didn't know what the future would bring, especially because of the unre- vealed letters, but it was enough to be here for the moment and to know that Mac and Trent no longer mistrusted her.

There had been no overt apologies, no verbal acknowledgment that Jesse had lied repeatedly, but she sensed in Trent and Mac a softening, a willingness to listen.

Soon, maybe tonight or tomorrow, she would pull Trent aside and show him the letters, even if it meant finding out that Allen wasn't a Sinclair. Trent, as Mac's eldest son, would have to make the decision about whether or not to let Mac see what his ex-wife had written to Jesse. And after that, who knew what would happen.

They pulled in to the parking lot of the small Jackson Hole airport and parked. Mac stayed in the car, but Trent and Bryn got out and leaned on the hood, hands over their eyes as they watched for landing aircraft. Prop planes were common. Occasionally a larger, commercial airliner.

But it was the sleek, small jet with the blue-and-green stripe and the Sinclair logo that caught Trent's attention. "That's it," he said. He tapped on the window. "C'mon, Dad."

Bryn walked on shaky legs, Trent and Mac at her side. This was more than just a normal visit. A new Sinclair was about to step foot onto the land of his heritage. And if he wasn't a Sinclair by blood, he was still Jesse's son.

She waited impatiently in the small concourse. Another jet had landed moment's before, and Bryn had to clench her fists and bide her time as the stream of tourists meandered inside from the tarmac.

At last Bryn saw the familiar outline of Aunt Beverly's gray head, with its short, tight curls. Her heart leaped in her chest. An unfamiliar woman in a white uniform walked at Beverly's side, but it was the third member of the entourage who spotted Bryn first and shouted at the top of his lungs.

Allen broke free of Beverly's hold and, despite her admonitions to go slowly, raced forward. "Mommy, Mommy!" His face was aglow.

She ran to meet him, scooping him up in a tight hug as she went to her knees. "Hello, my little sweetheart. I've missed you so much." He smelled of sweat and peanut butter and little boy.

He suffered through a moment of Bryn scattering kisses on his freckled cheeks, but then pulled away impatiently, already asserting his manly independence even in the middle of a reunion. His skin was pale. Dark smudges beneath his eyes emphasized his pallor, but he had certainly recovered his high spirits.

"Who are they, Mommy?" He tugged her to her feet and looked past her with curiosity.

Tears clogged her throat and she had to try twice to speak. "That's Trent and his father, Mr. Sinclair." She lowered her voice to a whisper. "Remember how I taught you to shake hands."

Allen grinned at the two strange males, his head cocked slightly to one side as he held out his tiny palm. "Very nice to meetcha."

Trent stood silent, unmoving, his features carved in stone.

Mac rubbed a hand across his face. "Oh, my God." He took Allen's outstretched hand and pumped it. "Welcome to Wyoming, son."

Eleven

After that, chaos reigned. They all made their way outside. Aunt Beverly and Allen were installed in the backseat with Bryn. Trent hadn't missed a trick. The booster seat he had purchased for Allen was exactly the correct size and model.

The nurse rode behind in a rental car with a hired driver. All the bags went with her, as well.

By the time the caravan got back to the ranch, Bryn was frazzled. Allen was hyperexcited,

Aunt Beverly was exhausted and Trent had yet to say more than a couple of terse words to anybody.

Mac was the one to show the new arrivals to their quarters and to help Bryn get everyone settled in. She was pleased that Allen's room was so close to hers. Even with two other caregivers watching out for him—one highly trained—she liked knowing that her son was where she could check on him during the night.

Lunch was quick and simple, sandwiches and fruit. Allen begged to explore the ranch, but the three women who controlled his fate insisted on a nap.

Mac took pity on the boy. He smiled down at him, his eyes misty. "How about I tell you a couple of stories about your—" He stopped short, sending Bryn a visual SOS. His face creased in distress.

She ruffled her son's blond hair, automatically trying to smooth the eternal cowlick. "Mac raised four sons on this ranch, Allen. Trent was one of them. I'll bet Mac can tell you lots of great stories about the trouble they got into."

That seemed to convince Allen, and the old man and the young boy wandered down the hall to Allen's new bedroom.

Which left Bryn and Aunt Beverly alone in the kitchen. Trent had disappeared, and the nurse was taking a much-deserved hour for herself.

Beverly hugged Bryn for the dozenth time. "I missed you, honey. The house was empty without you."

"I missed you, too. Did Allen really do okay... until he got sick?"

"He was a sweetheart." Beverly eased into a chair at the table. "I'm stiff from the plane ride, even if it was the equivalent of being treated like a queen. Good grief, Bryn. These folks have some serious money. They should have been helping you all these years."

Bryn bent her head. "It was complicated." Aunt Beverly knew most of the story, though she had no clue that Bryn had harbored a crush on Trent. She sat down beside her aunt. "Mac hasn't said so, but I can tell from his face that he thinks Allen is Jesse's son. He practically melted, just like a doting granddad should."

Beverly extended her feet, clad in sensible walking shoes, and stretched. "How long will we be staying?"

Panic welled in Bryn's chest. Mac was back in fighting form. Once Allen had a chance to immerse himself in ranch life and the nurse declared him fully recovered, there would no longer be any reason for Bryn and her son to stay.

Which meant Bryn had to confront Trent with the letters. Soon.

And that was problematic, because Trent had reverted to the coolly reserved, impossible-to-read man she had first encountered in Mac's sickroom when she arrived. She no longer detected hostility from him, but his utter lack of emotion was even worse.

He either refused to believe the evidence of

his own eyes, or he had no interest in getting to know his nephew.

When Allen woke from a long nap, he was grumpy, but a juice box and a cookie soothed him. The nurse checked him over, and soon, Mac and Bryn were on horseback, with Allen—wearing a mask as a precaution—riding in front of his grandfather. They covered a lot of ground, and Mac's transformation was miraculous. No longer an invalid, he was suddenly hale and hearty again, his skin a healthy color and his eyes sparkling with enthusiasm.

At one point when Allen was occupied playing with puppies on the front porch, Mac took Bryn's arm. "We need to talk this evening."

Bryn nodded solemnly, a lump in her throat. "Okay. After I get Allen settled for the night, I'll come find you."

"Trent will need to be there, also."

She nodded again, but couldn't think of a thing to say. Trent's feelings on the subject of Jesse's son were an unknown quantity.

Allen tired quickly. They whisked him back to the house and Beverly occupied him with a simple board game while Bryn talked to the nurse. The prognosis was promising. They would have to be vigilant about inhalers and the like, but there was a very good chance Allen would outgrow the worst of his asthma.

After dinner Allen was allowed to watch one of his favorite Disney DVDs, and then it was bedtime.

When Bryn entered Mac's office a short while later, he was already there. And so was Trent. Mac greeted her with a smile. Trent barely noticed that she'd entered the room. He sat in front of the computer, his forehead creased in concentration as he studied the screen.

For a moment she flashed back to that dreadful day six years ago. But she was not here to plead her own case on this occasion. She was an advocate for her son. Bryn wanted nothing for herself from the Sinclairs unless it was freely given. Not money, not love, not anything.

Mac motioned for her to sit in the big, comfy armchair. It was a man's chair, and it dwarfed her, but she complied. Still, Trent remained apart from the conversation. Mac reached in a drawer and pulled out a five-by-seven silver frame.

He handed it to Bryn. She stared at it, but it took a few moments for understanding to click. The birthday cake in the picture was decorated with five candles. And the gap-toothed birthday boy with the wide grin and the cowlick was Jesse.

He could have been Allen's twin. Her throat tightened. "I don't know what to say."

Mac's eyes glazed with wetness, but he coughed and tried to cover his emotion. "I think you know how sorry we are for what happened six years ago, but Trent and I want to make a formal apology and ask you to forgive us. Isn't that right, Trent?"

Finally, Trent revolved and faced her, his expression unreadable. "Yes, of course."

Bryn squirmed in the chair, bringing her knees up beside her in an effort to get comfortable. For years she had thought an apology was what she wanted, but now that the time had arrived, she realized that it changed nothing. "I appreciate the thought," she said slowly. "But I understand why you did what you did, especially Trent. Jesse was the light of this family...the heart and soul. You all poured your love into him, and it would never have occurred to you that he was capable of such bare-faced lies."

Mac scowled. "Trent can be absolved on that account, but even back then I realized that Jesse's sweetness and compliance was an act. I was trying to protect him and you, too, Bryn. But I handled it badly. If I had encouraged you to stay and had challenged Jesse to own up to the truth, I'm convinced that things would have gotten very ugly, very fast."

"So you sent me to Beverly."

"Your mother spoke highly of her older sister, and after you ran out of the study that day, I contacted Beverly to explain the situation. We both agreed that you needed to be with a woman during your pregnancy." He came over to the chair and laid a hand on her shoulder. "But it wasn't that I didn't love you, darlin'. I never stopped loving you."

Bryn reached up to stroke his hand. "Thank you, Mac. And I'm sorry I was such a brat and sent all your presents back."

He grinned. "They're in a closet in my bedroom. You're welcome to them."

Her eyebrows went up. "Ooh...an early Christmas. I might have to take you up on that."

Mac sobered. "Allen is your son, and any decisions about his future are up to you. But I want you to know that I already have my lawyers preparing the paperwork to make him a legitimate heir to my estate."

Bryn looked at Trent, begging him without words to say something, anything.

He was stoic, watchful.

Her stomach churned with tension. What did Trent's silence mean? Was he angry? Would he challenge the will?"

She straightened. "I assume you'll want to do DNA testing to establish the relationship between Jesse and Allen."

Mac snorted. "Allen's a mirror image of Jesse at that age. Any fool can see it. I don't think we need a test."

At long last, Trent spoke up. "It might be important to the boy one day to have the proof positive. So no one can ever doubt him."

Bryn's heart sank. Trent still wasn't sure she was telling the truth. "Does this mean you don't believe me, Trent?" She had to know.

Impatience darkened his features. "Of course I believe you, Bryn. Even before I saw the boy I believed you. But I deal in legalities, and it never hurts to dot the *i's* and cross the *t's*."

She nibbled her lower lip, not at all certain what was going on inside his head. It seemed as though he couldn't even bring himself to say Allen's name. Was he angry that Bryn had borne Jesse's child?

Mac raked a hand through his thick silver hair. "Today was a big day, and I'm almost as wiped out as the kid. I'll say good night. See you both in the morning."

His departure left an awkward silence in the room. Bryn had hoped to approach Trent in a better mood when she revealed the letters, but the time had run out. No wills could be notarized, nor big declarations made, until the truth about the letters from Etta came to light.

She took a deep breath. "Trent, there's something I need to show you. Something important."

He lifted an eyebrow. "What is it?"

"It will be easier if I show you. It will only take me a minute. Please wait here."

His gaze followed her out of the room, and

she went rapidly to extract the shoe box from its hiding place.

When she returned, Trent hadn't moved. His eyes narrowed suspiciously. "What is that?"

She held the box to her chest. "Not long after I arrived—the day you took your dad to the doctor and I was here alone—I realized that Jesse's room had not been cleaned since his death. I did some laundry...straightened up the mess. And in the process, I found a box of letters written to him by Etta. As far as I can tell, they started arriving about the time he turned sixteen."

Trent's eyes blazed with emotion, and he took the box from her hands with a jerk. "Let me see that."

She hated showing them to him, knowing it would cause him pain. "They're bad, Trent... wicked in cases...and cruel. Perhaps Jesse's self-destructive behavior was being fueled by something none of us knew anything about."

Trent reclaimed his original seat at the desk

and opened the box. He riffled through the contents for maybe ten seconds before selecting an envelope and extracting the enclosed piece of notepaper. As he read it, his scowl blackened.

She could only imagine what he was thinking. She, herself, had been shocked and dismayed the first time she had read the letters. How much worse would it be for Trent, knowing that his own mother had been so intentionally mean-spirited?

No, it was actually worse than that. A child was supposed to be able to know that his parents loved him unconditionally. Jesse would have been better off thinking that his mother had left for parts unknown and was never coming back. Desertion was a terrible blow to a vulnerable boy. But in writing the series of notes designed to manipulate Jesse's fragile emotions, Etta had moved from abandonment to deliberate harm.

Trent read every word of every letter. Bryn sat in silence as the clock ticked away the minutes. The house was quiet. Everyone else had gone to bed. Trent's face was terrible to see. His shoulders slumped, his skin grayed, his lips tightened.

When he finished the last one and turned to face her, his eyes were damp. She had expected him to be angry...and perhaps that would come...later. But at this precise moment, he was in so much pain, he was unable to hide it, even from her.

He swallowed hard. "Why? Why would she do such a thing?"

Bryn clasped her hands in her lap, searching in vain for the right words to ease the torment etched on his face. "I don't know, Trent. Maybe she thought that if she could worm her way back into Jesse's life, Mac would let her come home."

He dropped his head in his hands, elbows on his thighs. "Jesse must have been so confused, so torn. He adored Dad, but she insinuated—"

Trent had seen it, too. Bryn squeezed the arms of the chair. "Etta made it sound as if

Mac wasn't Jesse's father." The words scraped her throat raw. "And if that is true, then Allen is not a Sinclair. Not at all."

Trent was so still, he worried her. She went to him and put her arms around his neck from behind. "I'm so sorry," she whispered, putting her cheek to his. "She was your mother. I know this hurts."

He shrugged out of her embrace and got up to pace, his hands shoved in his pockets. She took the seat he had vacated and wrapped her arms around her waist, trying not to let him see how upset she was. Trent had enough to deal with at the moment without comforting her.

Intense emotion blasted the air in unseen waves. He ranged around the small space like an animal trapped in a cage. He paused finally and leaned against the wall, fatigue in every line of his posture. "Why didn't you show them to me when you first found them?" he asked dully.

"I was afraid. Afraid of hurting Mac...hurting you."

"Afraid of losing your quarter of the Sinclair fortune?"

Her actions hadn't been blameless. She shouldn't have been surprised by the question. But Trent's question sliced through her composure and left her bleeding.

"Fair enough. I understand why it might look that way. But I was always going to show you these eventually. I had to. You deserved that from me. Because sometimes the only way to help with grief is to find answers."

"Did you think about destroying the letters?"

"No," she said bluntly. "I would have had to live with guilt for the rest of my life. I *want* Allen to be a Sinclair, but only if it's true. If Jesse was not Mac's son, we'll deal with it somehow."

"You didn't show these to Mac." It was a statement, not a question.

"No. He's been so frail. I did wonder if maybe he knew about them already. They weren't exactly hidden. The box fell off the top shelf in the closet when I was putting things away."

"But Mac wouldn't have snooped in Jesse's room."

"No, I guess not."

They both fell silent.

When Trent didn't say anything more, apparently lost in thought, she pressed him. "Do you think we should show them to him now? He's like a new man since Allen came."

Trent frowned. "True. But if he *didn't* know about them, then the contents might give him another heart attack. And I don't know if I can risk that."

"We can't let him change the will if he's not Allen's grandfather. It would be wrong… unethical…"

"But if bringing Allen into the family makes Mac happy, who are we to stand in the way?"

It was her turn to frown, her stomach knotted.

"You made it clear six years ago that being a Sinclair is a bond all of you shared, and I didn't. My growing up here meant nothing. So what would make you soften that stance now?"

Trent's expression was inscrutable, his mouth a grim line. "Six years ago I hadn't lost my baby brother to a drug addiction. Six years ago I hadn't watched my father nearly die of a heart attack. Six years ago, I was a self-centered jackass."

His unaccustomed humility made her uneasy. She counted on Trent to be a rock. She didn't need his self-abnegation. Not now. Not with so much riding on the outcome of the next several days.

She glanced at her watch. The hours had flown. It was midnight—the witching hour. That dark moment when everything bad in life was magnified into a crushing burden. No longer able to sit still, she stood up and went to the window, her back to Trent.

Her breath fogged up the chilled glass. "So

what do we do?" She wanted him to come to her, take her in his arms and tell her everything would be all right.

But as always, Trent was not a man to be easily understood or bent to a woman's will. She sensed him watching her, but he remained where he was. "I have to think," he said gruffly. "Too much is at stake to make any snap decisions. Will the boy take a nap tomorrow?"

The boy. Trent still couldn't say her son's name. "Yes." She drew a heart in the condensation on the windowpane.

"Then let's you and I take a ride in the afternoon. We'll go to the far side of the meadow… where the creek cuts through the aspen. No one will interrupt us. We'll talk and decide what to do."

Trent was speaking matter-of-factly. Nothing in his tone or demeanor suggested a hint of passion. But unbidden, her mind jumped to memories of the night they'd shared in the cabin, and she felt her face heat. It might as well have been happening again at this very instant, so vivid was the recollection of each perfect minute.

Her moans and cries. His hoarse shouts. The rustle of the straw beneath the quilt. The snap and pop of the fire. The comforting drone of rain on the metal roof.

His touch lingered on her skin. She breathed in his crisp masculine scent. His hard body moved over her and in her. Soft sighs, ragged murmurs...pleasure so deep and swift-running she drowned in it.

She was glad they weren't facing each other. Her face would have given her away. She stiffened her spine, drawing on every ounce of self-possession she could muster. She turned to look at him and almost flinched at the intensity of his gaze.

For one blazing instant she saw raw, naked hunger beyond comprehension in his narrow gaze. A predatory declaration of intent. But he blinked, and it was gone.

Had she imagined it? Did he still desire her,

or had her actions in concealing the letters destroyed the fragile bond between them?

She bit her lower lip, unsure how to proceed.

Trent's posture had relaxed somewhat. He leaned against the wall, looking tired and discouraged. Seeing him so vulnerable hurt her somewhere deep in her chest. He had taken on so much responsibility in the last few weeks. And her revelation about the letters, necessary though it was, had only added to the load he carried.

She toyed with the cord that controlled the wide-slatted wooden blinds, unable suddenly to meet his gaze. "I'll be glad to go with you tomorrow," she said quietly. "To talk things through. But in the end, it has to be your decision, Trent. Mac is your father. You know what's best for him and your family. I think he could help us get to the bottom of Etta's correspondence and what it means. But if you think he can't handle it, we'll destroy them and no one will be the wiser."

He ran a hand through his rumpled hair. "This is a hell of a mess. I need to call Gage and Sloan."

"Can they come back so soon?"

"Gage is due here in a week anyway, because we all agreed to give the old man a month of our time to help get things at the ranch back up and running. And Sloan, well, I'm pretty sure he'd come back under the circumstances. They deserve to know the truth about Jesse's problems, but I don't know if we can wait to talk to Dad about the letters."

It hit her suddenly that Trent was planning to leave…and soon. His month was up. He'd be going back to Denver. Without her. She'd known it was going to happen…eventually. But she had deliberately closed her mind to the thought of it. It hurt too much.

She went to him and laid her head on his

chest, circling her arms around his waist. "I'm so sorry, Trent."

His hand came up to stroke her hair. Beneath her cheek she felt his heart thundering like a freight train. "Go to bed," he said softly. "Get some rest. I'll see you in the morning."

Twelve

Trent saddled his horse and headed out, following the route he and Bryn had taken to the cabin. But tonight Trent pushed his mount, skirting the edge of recklessness, trying to outrun the barrage of thoughts whirling in his brain. Every word of the damn letters was emblazoned in his memory. And it hurt. After all these years, his mother's betrayal hurt.

And then there was Bryn. What was he going to do about Bryn? From the moment he'd set eyes on Allen, he'd been consumed by guilt. The kid was Jesse's son, no question. Yet, six years ago they had thrown Bryn out in the street. Like she was some sort of sinner. And all along, Jesse had stood by and let it happen.

Dammit. What an unholy mess.

Trent couldn't lie to himself any longer. He was head over heels in love with Bryn. And it wasn't something that was going to magically go away. Hell, he'd been half in love with her for years. She was his heart, the very essence of who he was. And whatever it took, he couldn't lose her.

He'd been an ass about Allen. He didn't know much about children, and the fact that the boy was Jesse's son hit Trent hard. He was only the uncle, but the bare truth was, he wanted to be the boy's father. And if Jesse wasn't Mac's son... Good God.

And still he rode on, paying penance, seeking answers, looking for absolution.

Bryn barely slept. Every time she rolled over to look at the illuminated dial of the clock, only an hour had passed…sometimes less. Her whole life hung in the balance. For years she had assumed that her son would one day take his place as a Sinclair. And she had believed that such a moment would cement the fact, once and for all, that the ranch would always be her home, no matter where she actually chose to live.

Deep in her soul she recognized a connection to the land here. Perhaps it was unwarranted. Her parents had been no more than hired help on the Sinclair ranch. But that reality couldn't change the way she felt.

And Trent…dear, complicated Trent. She loved him beyond reason. Loved him enough to know that no other man would ever measure up. She didn't want to spend her life alone, but it would take a long, long time to forget the imprint Trent had made on her soul.

Jesse might have been the one who took her virginity, but Trent had showed her what it meant to be a woman.

An early morning walk calmed some of her

agitation and made it possible for Bryn to greet her son and aunt across the breakfast table with some degree of equanimity. Beverly and the nurse carried on a lively conversation. Mac's mood was jovial, and no one remarked on Trent's absence. An empty cereal bowl and coffee cup were evidence that he'd been up early.

Allen finished off his pancakes and turned, bright-eyed, toward his mom. "What are we going to do today?"

Bryn had thought about letting him explore the attic—she'd loved doing that as a child— but she worried that the dust might aggravate his asthma. He wasn't going to be content with puzzles and board games now that he was feeling better. Inspiration hit her. "Come with me," she said. "I have a surprise for you."

With Allen bouncing along beside her, she went to the large family room and opened the cabinet that stored all the leather-bound picture albums. Gage, Mac's second son, had developed a passion for photography early in life, and

Mac had indulged him with fancy and expensive cameras, lenses and developing equipment. Mac could never have imagined in those early days how Gage's love of photography, combined with a strong wanderlust, would take him to far-flung places across the globe.

Bryn opened one of the early albums and spread it in Allen's lap. Her throat tightened as she recognized a long-forgotten photo. It was one of the rare instances where Gage was actually "in" the picture, and Mac had been the photographer. Five children, four boys and a girl, sat on the top corral rail, their legs dangling. The three older brothers bore a striking resemblance, though Trent, probably twelve or thirteen, stood out as the eldest.

Bryn and Jesse sat side by side with the bigger kids, their arms around each other's shoulders. Bryn's hair was in pigtails…Jesse's blond head gleamed in the morning sun. All five children looked healthy, happy and carefree.

When Allen wasn't looking, Bryn took the

photo and slipped it in her pocket. Soon, very soon, she'd tell him about his father. And she wouldn't lie, if possible. There were plenty of good memories to share.

She flipped the pages...showing Allen a montage of county rodeos, family Christmases, impromptu picnics on the ranch...all chaperoned by a much younger Mac. Allen drank it all in with avid interest.

The final album was smaller than the rest. Inside the front cover was a faded Post-it note in Mac's handwriting that read *For Bryn*. Every photo inside was of her parents, sometimes together, sometimes smiling alone for the camera, many times holding their little girl.

She touched one picture she barely remembered. "That's my mom and dad," she said softly. "I wish you could have known them. But they died a long time before you were born."

A frown creased Allen's small forehead. "Did my daddy die, too? Is that why he doesn't live with us?"

The question came out of the blue and took her breath away. Allen had never once asked about his father. Bryn had been prepared for some time now to launch into an explanation when Allen seemed old enough to understand, but until today, he'd never questioned their non-traditional family.

She had lain many nights, sleepless, wondering how to explain to a small child that his father didn't want him. Now she didn't have to.

She swallowed the lump in her throat, desperately wanting to point to a photo of Jesse and say, "That was your dad." But she couldn't. Not yet. Not until things were settled.

"Yes," she said simply. "Your father died. But he loved you very much." Perhaps God would forgive her for the lie. A son needed to know that his father thought the world of him. Even if it wasn't true.

In the way of five-year-olds, Allen suddenly lost interest in the past. "Can we go see the puppies now?" he asked, wheedling in every syllable of his childish plea.

"You bet." She laughed. "I'll get Julio to bring them up from the barn."

Lunch was a scattered affair. Bryn and Allen took sandwiches out into the sunshine to eat, spreading a quilt on the ground and enjoying their alfresco meal. It had been a long, hard winter in Minnesota, and the spring warmth was too appealing to resist. But by one o'clock, Allen was flagging. Bryn turned him over to Beverly and the nurse.

When she left her son's bedroom, Trent appeared suddenly in the hallway, his expression somber. "Are you ready?"

She nodded, her stomach flip-flopping with nerves. "Yes."

One of the ranch hands insisted on helping Bryn saddle her horse, though she could have done it on her own. Trent mounted a beautiful stallion and waited for her to put a foot in the stirrup and leap astride the gentle mare assigned to her. She was self-conscious about Trent watching her, but she managed not to embarrass herself.

They rode side by side in silence, crossing a meadow bursting with flowers and sporting new green in every shade. Trent had rolled up Bryn and Allen's luncheon quilt and tied it to the back of his saddle. He'd also brought along a couple of canteens of fresh water.

When they reached the creek, Trent helped her dismount and tied both animals to trees so the horses could eat and drink as needed. He spread the faded blanket and dropped the canteens to anchor the fabric against the capricious breeze.

Nearby, the crystal-clear, frigid water burbled gently over smooth stones that were as old as the mountains themselves. Trent faced her, his expression unreadable.

The breeze tossed her hair in her face. She took a rubber band from her pocket and bound the flyaway mess at the base of her neck. "Where do we start?" she asked. The calm in her voice was a complete fabrication. Her knees were the consistency of jelly, and her heart fluttered in her chest.

Trent took one step in her direction. "With this," he said gruffly. He took her in his arms, and instantly her fear and anxiety melted away to be replaced by heat and certainty. It was a homecoming, a benediction, a warm, wicked claiming.

Did he know? Did he have any idea that she was his in every way that mattered? She met the urgency of his kiss eagerly. The hunger that consumed both will and reason no longer frightened her.

She would have followed him into hell for the chance to have him again, to know the searing touch of his hands on her damp flesh.

He was inside her jeans, his big hands cupping her bottom, drawing her tight against the hard, pulsing ridge of his erection.

"Trent. Oh, Trent." She wanted to say more, needed to say more. But it was all she could do to remain standing.

They ripped at clothing, hers and his, unashamed to be naked beneath the gentle afternoon sun. Bits of shade dappled their bare skin.

She barely noticed when he drew her to the soft caress of the quilt. He went down on his back, taking any discomfort from the rocky ground and making it his, while she sat cradled astride his hard thighs.

His thick, eager erection was impossible to miss. It lifted boldly between them, filled with life and purpose.

The gleam in his eyes made her blush. "Stop that," she hissed, unable to hold his gaze. She looked around, knowing they were alone, but feeling bashful nevertheless.

He gently traced the curve of one breast, lingering to coax the nipple to hardness. "Stop what?"

The innocence in his question might have been more convincing if he hadn't simultaneously brushed his finger in the wetness between her legs. Where his touch trespassed, her body went lax and soft, ready to take him. Eager for more.

She cleared her throat. "I thought we were going to talk," she said. It seemed as though one of them should make an effort to be sensible, but it was difficult for a woman to be taken seriously when she was sprawled in erotic abandon beneath a cloudless sky.

A shadow darkened his face for scant seconds, but he shook it off, his hands clenching her hips hard enough to bruise.

"Later," he groaned, rolling on a condom and lifting her to align their bodies. "Watch us," he muttered. "Don't close your eyes."

He entered her inch by inch, and though she squirmed and shivered, her gaze never wavered from the spot where his hard flesh penetrated her. The act was as elemental as the cry of the hawk overhead, as life-affirming as the advent of new life in the wild.

He filled her completely, his mighty arms straining as he lifted her repeatedly. Her knees burned, her thighs ached. The intentionally lazy tempo drove her mad with longing. She bore down on him, squeezing, pressing his shaft so he would go faster.

But Trent Sinclair had an iron will, and his control was frustrating for a woman whose patience unraveled with every upward thrust of his hips. She was so close to the moment of release, she held her breath.

Acting on instinct, she lightly touched his copper-colored nipples, circling them and making Trent flinch and groan hoarsely. Within her, he grew. Harder. Longer. More insistent.

She was stretched. Impaled. Held captive to the madness that drove them both to the brink of insanity. And it *was* insane. There was no future for them. No hope for a positive conclusion.

All they had was the present.

She put her hands on his shoulders. He reached behind her, and with a brutal twist of his fingers, snapped the band that held her ponytail. The long silky strands tumbled over her breasts and onto his chest. He stroked her hair with wonder and reverence in his gaze.

Then his hands fisted in the silken fall and he dragged her down so his mouth could ravage hers. Teeth and tongues and clashing breath. His sweat-slicked chest heaved, her thigh muscles quivered. He tortured them both, making them wait, drawing out the anticipation of the end until she wanted to scream at him and scratch his bronzed muscles with her fingernails, anything to hasten the promised pleasure that shimmered just out of reach.

He seized her face in his hands, his fingers sliding into the damp hair at her nape. His rapier gaze locked on hers. "You should have been mine, Bryn. He didn't deserve you. You should have been mine." Something in the rough, aching words made her heart hurt. But then he kissed her again, and the joy returned.

They were helpless, lost in the windswept eroticism of the moment. He laughed at her, laughed at them both. Nothing could have torn them apart. She lay on his chest, exhausted. The new angle sent tingling sensations from her core throughout her body.

His strength and stamina amazed her. He grunted and thrust more wildly. She was limp in his embrace, desperately aroused, but unable to summon the energy to sit up again.

"Tell me you want me, Bryn. I need to hear you say it." He rolled them suddenly, coming on top of her, but bearing most of his weight on his forearms.

She licked her lips, her throat parched. "I want you."

"Tell me you need me."

"I need you."

"I wish I had been your first."

Her slight hesitation sent lightning flashing in his dark gaze, dangerous, potent.

"I was immature," she said softly. "I think I used him to make you jealous. And I am so sorry for that. But I was never *in love* with Jesse."

She waited for him to say he loved her. Prayed with incoherent desperation that he would say the words that would change her life forever. The simple phrase that would make all her dreams come true.

But no such words were forthcoming.

Trent's face was unreadable. He was a man in the throes of passion...nothing in his features to express anything other than a dominant drive toward completion.

And finally, when she was boneless in his embrace, he rode her hard and took his own release with a ragged shout that echoed across the plain.

Trent pulled the edge of the quilt around the sleeping woman in his arms and checked his watch. The minutes ran away from him like rivulets of water on a rain-soaked windowpane. He wanted to preserve this slice of time, keep it pristine in his memory. But the moment of reckoning was fast approaching and it might be very ugly indeed. No matter how much he wanted to protect Bryn and her son from pain, his efforts might be futile.

He closed his eyes, feeling the sun burn into the skin of his eyelids and face.

He stroked her hair, abashed to realize that he was no longer jealous of his dead brother. Jesse had held Bryn like this…had made love to her. The knowledge was painful. But he loved his brother. Would always love him. And Jesse's premature death was a tragedy that would forever mark their family.

He was hard again. It seemed to be a perpetual, inescapable condition in her presence. He shifted her gently onto her side so they were face-to-face. Carefully, he lifted her leg across his hip. Breathing hard, he probed gently at her swollen entrance.

Bryn murmured, and the ghost of a smile teased her lips as her eyelids fluttered and opened. He pushed until he was seated fully in her still-slick passage. He moved slowly, savoring the way her body grasped his shaft. She felt small and fragile in his embrace, but she was strong in ways he could never match. She'd made a home for her son as a single mother.

Beverly had been a source of strength... true. But Bryn was a good mother, a woman of backbone and grit, much like the pioneer females who helped settle the wild and dangerous West.

She kissed him and murmured soft words of pleasure. He gritted his teeth as his climax bore down on him. He'd taken her like a crazy man less than a half hour before, and already he was at the edge again.

He slowed his strokes, relishing the position that enabled him to kiss her as he moved in and out with deliberate thrusts. Dark smudges beneath her eyes tugged at his heartstrings. Sleepless nights. Endless worry. But her smile was pure sunshine.

When he thought of the way he and Mac had thrown her out six years ago—a naive, pregnant eighteen-year-old—he was sickened. He'd never be able to make that up to her, but God knows, he could try.

He shuddered as his brain ceded control to his baser instincts. Tremors shook him. The base of his spine tightened.

"Bryn..." He spoke her name urgently, needing to see her forgiveness, wanting absolution.

She caught her breath. "Trent...ohh..."

Their position was intimate, sensual. He put his hand on the soft curve of her bottom and pulled her in to his downstroke. Her back arched. Her eyes closed. She was so beautiful, he was blinded. He told himself it was the sun.

But it was her. It was Bryn. Until she came

back to the ranch, he'd had no clue his life was an empty shell. But she had shown him the truth. And all she'd had to do was be herself… pure, generous, charming.

He'd been lost from the first moment, though he'd fought hard to believe she was a liar and a cheat. It was much easier that way.

He brushed a kiss across each of her cheeks, her nose, her eyelids. The urgent need for climax had retreated to a muted simmer. His primary emotion at the moment was quiet contentment. And for a man unused to examining something as hazy and insubstantial as feelings, it was a significant shock to realize that the woman in his arms was as necessary to him as breathing.

The knowledge was exhilarating and scary as hell.

He pushed her over onto her back and urged her legs around his waist. Her skin was soft and luminous in the unforgiving light of day. What would it have been like to be her pioneer husband, bound inside a tiny log cabin for weeks at a time as blizzards howled?

Isolation. Nothing to diffuse the interaction between male and female. Nothing to run interference when one of them was in a bad mood. Nowhere to escape when tempers flared.

He'd have taken her night after night, wrapped in a world of only two. And it would have been as close to heaven as a man like him was liable to get. He'd said Jesse didn't deserve her, but the truth was, neither did he.

She smiled at him, a secretive curve of soft pink lips that made him shake. Her gaze was slumberous. The look of a woman who had been well loved. Any man in his right mind would move heaven and earth to make her his. He'd grown up believing that everyone and everything had a price. But not Bryn. She had never asked for a single thing.

And he wanted to give her the world.

He moved in her, wanting to imprint his

touch on her heart so that she could never forget him.

She dug her heels into his lower back. "Whatever happens, Trent, I'll always remember this." Her gaze was solemn, melancholy.

He nuzzled her neck. "I'll work it out. Trust me."

A slight frown appeared between her perfectly arched brows. "Work what out?"

He withdrew almost completely and chuckled when she said an unladylike word. He dropped his head forward, resting his brow against hers. "Mac. Jesse. Allen. The letters. You'll see."

She tightened her legs around his waist with surprising strength. "Less talk. More action."

He tried to laugh, but it came out as a groan. He let it snap…the cord he'd bound so tightly around his need, his control. Again and again, he entered her, holding back until he heard her sharp cry and felt her body spasm around his rigid flesh. And then he buried his face in her neck and leaped into the unknown, feeling only the soft pillow of her breasts and knowing that there was nowhere else he wanted to be.

Sweat dried on their skin. The sun moved lower, brushing the mountains with gold and lavender.

He came so close to blurting out his love for her. But the habits of a lifetime were deeply ingrained. Never operate from a position of weakness. Make a plan. He'd get everything worked out in his head, and then he'd tell her. When the time was right.

Bryn was so silent and still beneath him, he felt panic tighten his throat.

He sat up and gathered her in his arms, warming her skin with his hands. The words rushed from his mouth, shocking the hell out of him. "Marry me, Bryn. Make Allen my son."

Thirteen

Over the years Bryn had entertained dozens of fantasies in which Trent declared his everlasting love for her, went down on one knee to offer her a ridiculously extravagant ring and begged her to marry him. None of those scripts bore any resemblance to what had just happened.

She stood up awkwardly, painfully aware of her nudity, and scrambled to pick up her clothes and put them on. In one quick glance she saw that Trent was frowning. No less magnificent and commanding in the buff than he was fully clothed, he stood with his hands on his hips.

When she was ready, she folded her arms across her waist and made herself look at him. She managed to swallow against a tight throat. "Thank you for asking," she said quietly, "but, no." He hadn't technically asked her at all. It had been more autocratic than that. An order. The mighty Trent Sinclair telling a minion what to do.

She hated that she was suspicious of his motives, but her instinct for self-preservation had kicked into high gear. She couldn't be one of his *acquisitions*. Her heart couldn't bear it.

Trent's scowl was black enough to make a grown man cower, but Bryn held her ground. His jaw was clenched so hard, the words bit out in sharp staccatos. "Why the hell not?"

The naive Bryn grieved for the ashes of fairy-tale romance. But practical Bryn had more to consider than hurt feelings. "If Allen is a Sinclair, then of course I want him to get to know his grandfather and you and Gage and Sloan and the ranch. But if it turns out that he's *not,* I'll take him back to Minnesota with me and we'll make a good life there with Beverly."

His eyes narrowed. "You said that whether or not to show Mac the letters was my decision. I say we destroy the damn things and move on... as a family."

The temptation to give in was overwhelming. She would be Trent's wife. Allen would be his son. There might be other children.

She bit her lip and shook her head. "I was wrong. I've had all night to think about it. Secrets are never the best course of action. Mac needs to know the truth. And afterward..."

He shoved his legs in his pants and buttoned his shirt. "And afterward, your son will either be very rich, or just another illegitimate kid being raised by a single parent."

She flinched. His deliberate cruelty shocked her. Was this his response to not getting his own way? "It's about more than the money," she whispered, her throat raw from the effort not to cry. "You know that."

He faced her, barefooted. Most people would appear vulnerable in that condition. Not Trent. "The world revolves around money, Bryn. And if you don't realize that, you're more of an innocent than I thought."

She was chilled to the bone though the day was warm. "Why are you being so hateful?" What had happened to tender, caring Trent? Had the gentler, kinder man been no more than a ruse to get her into bed?

He shrugged, the smile on his face mocking. "If I'm not in the best of moods, Brynnie, you'll have to take the blame for that. It's not every day I get a marriage proposal tossed back in my face. Forgive me if I'm not so cavalier about it as to go on with life as normal."

For the briefest flash of a second, she thought she saw hurt flicker in his cold gaze, but then it was gone. She couldn't hurt Trent. He was impervious, thick-skinned. That was the only way to make it to the top.

She bit her lip. "Why did you ask me to marry you?"

He propped his foot on a stone and bent to put on the left boot, then the right.... Was he hiding his expression deliberately? His voice was muffled. "We owe you. Maybe not Gage and Sloan, but certainly Jesse and Mac and I. You suffered at our hands, and that can't be erased. Sinclairs always repay their debts."

Disappointment and grief tangled in her stomach, destroying any last hope that Trent felt something for her beyond simple lust. "I absolve you," she said dully. "There's plenty of blame to go around. I kept Allen away from you all for five years. So let's call it even."

She picked up the quilt and rolled it with jerky motions. "I need to get back to the house."

The hours until Bryn and Trent could meet with Mac in private passed like molasses on a cold day. Allen's high spirits frayed Bryn's nerves, yet finally, by nine o'clock, Allen was sound asleep. Bryn didn't waste any time. She retrieved the box of letters and made her way to Mac's study.

The two men were already there.

Her heart thumping, she entered hesitantly, searching out Trent with her gaze to see if his face gave any indication of what was to come. What had he said to Mac? Anything? She sat down and waited.

Trent ran a hand over the back of his neck, looking uncustomarily frazzled. "How are you feeling, Dad?"

Mac frowned. "I'm great. What's all this about?"

At Trent's almost imperceptible nod, Bryn smiled wanly. "We have some things to tell you, but we don't want you to get upset."

Mac snorted and rolled his eyes. "I may have a contrary ticker, but I'm not some damned pansy who's going to wilt over a little bad news. For

God's sake, spit it out. You're making me nervous. You and Trent look like you've swallowed bad fish. Tell me what it is. Now."

Bryn gripped the box in her lap. When she looked at Trent, he was no help at all. He simply shrugged.

She stood up and moved to where Mac sat in the leather chair that was his version of a throne. "I found these," she said. "When I was cleaning Jesse's room. They're letters. From Etta. Did you know Jesse's mother had been writing to him?"

"God, no." Mac paled.

Bryn winced. "I was afraid of that. They're bad, Mac. She tried to poison his mind. And her deliberate mischief-making may have contributed to the drugs. Jesse would have been confused. And hurt."

"Let me see." He tried to take the box, but she held on to it for a moment more.

"That's not all." She was surprised she was

able to speak. Her throat spasmed painfully. "Jesse may not be your son."

Mac's big hands trembled. He jerked the box away from her. "Damn it, girl, quit coddling me."

The room was silent when Mac tossed the last letter in the box and replaced the lid. He set the innocent-looking cardboard container on the desk and laid his head against the back of his chair. His eyes were closed. Bryn was not in the mood to indulge him.

She got to her feet and paced. "Talk to us, Mac. Please."

He scrubbed his hands over his face and turned his head in her direction. His entire body had deflated. He looked like an old man.

Trent exhaled an audible breath. "Dad. Come clean with us. What's going on?"

Mac sighed. "I didn't know about the letters, but I've known where Etta was every day since she left."

Trent looked thunderstruck.

262 THE SECRET CHILD & THE COWBOY CEO

Bryn managed to speak. "I don't understand. I thought she ran away. Left her kids. Left you."

Mac nodded. "She did that for sure. And I checked her into a mental facility, because she had a complete, devastating breakdown. She split with reality. Etta has been a patient at the Raven's Rest Inpatient Facility in Cheyenne for almost two decades."

Trent gaped. "For God's sake, Dad. Why did you never tell us? Why did you let us think she ran away?"

"She did run away. At first. But when I found her, she was cowering in a bus station like a wounded wild animal." Mac's voice broke, and Bryn saw that even after all the years that had passed, he still loved her.

He continued, his voice thick. "I took her to the hospital. And she was never able to come back home. She was a danger to herself and others. There were a few good days here and there, but for the most part, she lives in an alternate world. I'm honestly shocked that she was able to remember Jesse well enough to be able to write to him."

"You think Jesse inherited some of her mental instability, don't you?" Trent's face had paled, as well.

Mac nodded slowly. "I wanted him to see someone…to get help…medication. Anything that he needed. But he never gave me an inch. Denial was his friend."

Bryn leaned forward. "So the other men she talks about in the letters? Did they exist?"

Mac's silence dragged on for tense moments. He was suddenly the epitome of an elderly man. "Yes." His tone was flat. "She never leaves the facility now. But before…when she was still living on the ranch…there were a couple of episodes. Jesse is probably not my biological son. I'd been gone for a few weeks to a cattle show. The timing…well…let's just say the odds are against it. But it doesn't matter anymore. Jesse is dead."

He got to his feet, almost stumbling, and leaned a hand on the back of the chair. "You were right to show me the letters. I'm sorry I didn't tell you the truth about your mother, Trent. But when you were all boys, I didn't want you to know. And by the time you were old enough to understand, I'd kept the secret so long, I couldn't bring myself to expose the truth."

He hugged his son, and Bryn was relieved to see that Trent gave as good as he got. She had feared he'd be furious. But whatever his emotions, he kept them in check for now.

Mac hugged Bryn, as well. "I love you, Brynnie, my girl. And you've always been family to me, with or without Jesse."

She kissed his cheek. "Sleep well, Mac. I'll check on you before I go to bed."

When it was just the two of them, Bryn studied Trent's face. He wasn't doing well. She could see it in his eyes, though he stood as proud as ever, his spine straight and his broad shoulders squared off against the world. She took his hand. "Come to the kitchen with me. I'll fix you something to drink. And I'll bet Beverly tucked away some of those sugar cookies."

He cocked his head, pulling his hand out of her grasp and stepping backward behind an invisible fence. "You don't have to pamper me. I'm not dying. But I guess you were smart to say no to my proposal. Who knows what crazy genes are rattling around inside me? I don't know which is worse—a mother who will abandon her children on a whim, or a raving maniac."

His sarcasm made her flinch. "Don't do that, Trent," she said urgently. "Give yourself time to process this. You've had a shock." She turned to Mac's desk. He'd been known to keep a flask for emergencies. "I'll pour you some whiskey. You deserve it after the day you've had."

Trent's laugh held little amusement as he took the tiny shot and tossed it back. He wiped his mouth with the back of his hand, his eyes bleak.

"There's not enough whiskey in the world to fix this."

"It will be okay," she said, trying to believe it.

It was as if he never heard her. "I'm going to have to be the one to call Gage and Sloan. I can't make Mac do it. He could barely tell me. Damn it to hell." Trent hurled the small glass against the wall and smiled with grim satisfaction when it shattered into a dozen pieces.

"You don't have to do anything tonight," she insisted. "It can wait until morning. When you've calmed down."

"I'm perfectly calm," he said, his tone blistering. "Go to bed, Bryn. This doesn't concern you."

"*You* concern me," she said. He was trying to hurt her…and he succeeded. But her own concerns had to be pushed aside temporarily for his sake. He needed to let go, let the anguish out, and hang on to someone else for a few minutes. But such perceived weakness wasn't in his repertoire. He was a Sinclair male. That particular animal was trained not to show weakness. Not to anyone.

She knelt to clean up the mess, and Trent barked at her.

"I said…go to bed." His eyes blazed in a white face.

She finished her task and dropped the pieces into the trash can. "I don't want to leave you right now. You need me."

He went still, and in that split second, she knew she had made a mistake. His lip curled. Any tenderness she'd ever imagined in his steely gaze had been obliterated by fury and suffering that was painful to witness.

"I don't *need* anyone, Brynnie. So leave me the hell alone."

Bryn gave herself and her son one last, precious twenty-four-hour period to enjoy the ranch. Their return flights, along with Beverly's and the nurse's, were booked for the following day.

She did her best to make her mind a blank. All that mattered now was ensuring that Allen and Mac spent time together and that Allen had one last opportunity to explore the ranch. She was the one making a decision to leave this time, but the end result was the same. She had to say goodbye to the two men she loved. And to the home where she had grown up with so many happy memories.

Allen ran circles around her when she lagged behind on their walk. Her sleepless night was catching up with her. She held up a hand. "Mommy needs to rest a minute." They were climbing a slight rise, and the two or three hours of sleep she'd had during the long, bleak night weren't enough to give her any energy at all.

She spied a boulder up ahead near the trail, one of many left behind when the glaciers retreated, and made a beeline for it. They were in sight of the house. Their trek had taken them in a big circle.

They sat down and Allen put his head in her lap, a move that said louder than words that he wasn't entirely back to normal. She stroked his hair. "I have something to tell you, sweetheart."

He yawned and swiped at his nose with a dirty hand. "Okay."

She hadn't expected it to be quite so hard. "You know how I told you I lived here when I was growing up?"

He nodded.

"Well, Mac had a son, Jesse, who was my age. I fell in love with him and that's how you were born."

"But my daddy died."

"Yes."

"Why didn't we live with him?"

This was the tricky part. Allen sat up and looked at her with big curious eyes. She bit her lip. "Ah, well…your dad was very sick and he couldn't help take care of a little boy."

Allen cocked his head. "Like strep throat?"

"No. Something that never got better. But you were very lucky because you had me and your aunt Beverly."

"Why didn't my dad ever invite me to come here?" Allen was sharp.

"He didn't want you to see him feeling bad. And he didn't tell Mac and Trent that you were his little boy. But now that they know, Mac wants you to visit as often as we can."

"Can we live here?"

Bryn groaned inwardly. "We already have a place to live…you know? And Aunt Beverly would miss us if we were gone."

Allen grinned. "Yeah. I guess." Then as usual, his focus shifted. "Can we go back to the house now? I'm hungry."

She ruffled his hair. "You're always hungry."

They took off at a trot, and Allen pretended

to race her, giggling when she panted and bent to put her hands on her knees. She took a deep breath and made one last sprint.

Two steps later, she cried out in shock when she stepped in a hole and her body kept going. There was a sickening crack, dreadful pain shot up her leg and she catapulted forward to meet the ground with a thud.

The first thing she remembered was her son's little hand patting her cheek. When she opened her eyes, she realized he was crying. "I'm okay," she said automatically.

He wasn't stupid. Fear painted his face. "Mommy, your phone's not in your pocket."

Oh, God. "I left it at the house." Throbbing pain made it difficult to enunciate.

"I'll go get help," he said, looking sober and not at all childlike.

"No. You'll get lost." She blurted it out, terrified at the possibility of letting her baby boy wander alone.

Allen took her face between his hands, his

expression earnest. "Mommy, I can see the house. It's over there."

He was right. The roof was visible through the trees. Her brain spun. What choice did she have? If she passed out—and it was a good possibility given the way she felt—she'd be leaving Allen unattended anyway. Was there any difference in the two scenarios? The pain made nausea rise in her throat as sweat beaded her forehead.

Desperately, she gazed at her small, brave son. "You must stay on the trail. And if you get confused, stop and come back. Be careful. Promise me."

He stood up. "I'll bring Trent, Mommy. He'll know what to do."

Trent was in the corral, examining the left rear shoe on his stallion, when a small figure out of the corner of his eye caught his attention. It was little Allen. Alone. Trent ran to meet him, his heart in his throat. "What happened? Where's your mother?" He dropped down on his knees, so the two of them were at eye level. Allen was wheezing a little bit, but his color was good. He was scared and trying hard not to show it.

He laid his head on Trent's shoulder in an innocent gesture of trust. "She stepped in a hole. Her ankle might be broken. I can show you where she is. It's not far."

Trent's brain buzzed. He scooped the little boy into his arms and tucked him up on the horse. "Hold on to the saddle horn. We're going to ride fast." Allen's eyes were huge, but he nodded. Trent put a foot in the stirrup and vaulted up behind him. "Let's go. I'm counting on you to show me the way...."

One arm wrapped around Allen's waist, Trent rode hell for leather. Thinking about Bryn, hurt and alone, made him crazy, so he did his best to concentrate on getting to her as quickly as he could.

Thankfully, the kid was right. It was less than a quarter of a mile. But when they reached

Bryn, she was unconscious. Trent felt his world wobble and blur. She had to be okay. She had to be okay. She had to.

He jumped down and set the boy on his feet. While Allen hovered anxiously, Trent took a handkerchief from his pocket and wet it with water from the canteen on the ground beside Bryn. He wiped her face gently. "Wake up, Bryn. I'm here. Wake up, sweetheart."

It was a full minute before Bryn responded. She was ghostly white, and her lips were pale. "You came."

The words were so low he had to bend his head to hear them. He reached out his hand for Allen, pulling him close. "Your son is a hero," he said softly. "I'd never have known where you were without him."

She tried to wet her lips. "I've hardly seen you speak to him. I thought you were angry because he was Jesse's son," she whispered, her voice almost inaudible.

He lifted the canteen to her lips and made her

drink. "Angry?" Had she hit her head after all? She wasn't making sense.

"Because he's not yours and mine."

It was his turn to frown. "Don't be ridiculous. I love Allen. He's my flesh and blood. I'll always love him."

It was a nightmare ride that took far longer than it should. The sun dropped lower in the sky as they made their halting way back toward the house.

When they finally reached the edge of the corral, Trent barked out orders, and ranch hands came running. Beverly took charge of Allen, and the nurse was at Trent's side as he carried Bryn into the house. He put her in his bedroom. It was larger and more comfortable than hers, with a massive king-size bed. Bryn moaned as he laid her carefully on the embroidered, navy silk duvet.

There was really no choice what to do. The ankle was clearly broken. The nurse confirmed

Trent's amateur diagnosis. Mac summoned a helicopter and Trent and the nurse boarded with Bryn for the brief trip to Jackson Hole.

Fourteen

"How is she, son?" Mac, Beverly and Allen had lingered at the ranch for a couple of hours, not wanting Allen to get restless at the hospital during what could be a lengthy surgery.

"She should be coming out of recovery any minute now." Trent was hollow inside, feeling the aftermath of adrenaline. The sterile waiting room had been a cage he'd prowled for several hours. "Why don't you go on in so she can see Allen first thing. It's room 317. I'm going to grab some coffee and a sandwich."

He didn't linger at the snack machine. It was almost nine and he knew Mac and Beverly wouldn't want to keep Allen out too late.

When he approached the room a quarter hour later, he could hear Allen's excited chatter and Bryn's softer voice. He drew in a sharp breath, swamped with a wave of relief to hear concrete proof that she was okay.

He hovered in the hall, wanting to give the others plenty of time to reassure themselves that Bryn had come through the surgery with no ill effects. Finally, the door opened, and Bryn's visitors exited. The nurse would ride back to the ranch with them.

Mac squeezed his shoulder. "Take care of our girl."

Now Bryn was alone. Trent took a deep breath, knocked briefly on the partially open door and stepped into the room.

Bryn shifted in the bed and winced. Even with really wonderful drugs, her ankle throbbed mercilessly.

When Trent appeared in the doorway, her heart jumped. She hoped he couldn't tell on the monitor. She was in pain. It had been a terrible, stressful day. And she felt in no condition to hold her own with him.

He looked like hell. "You should have gone home with the others," she said quietly. "You're exhausted."

He pulled up a chair beside her bed. "I'm not leaving you." His angular face was creased with fatigue, his eyes shadowed. She wanted to smooth a hand over his hair, but she felt the invisible wall between them.

"There's no need for you to stay. I'm fine... really." She touched the neck of her hospital gown and sighed inwardly. Her hair was a mess. She would kill for a shower. And Trent had to see her like this. It wasn't fair. She always seemed to be at a disadvantage when it came to their interactions.

He took her hand in his, examining the shallow cuts and scrapes that covered the palm. She had tried to catch herself when she fell. It was a wonder she hadn't broken an arm. He ran his thumb gently over the worst of the wounds. "I lost ten years off my life today."

He looked at her, for once his dark gaze completely unguarded, and her breath caught in her chest. Was she imagining the agonized concern she saw there?

She curled her fingers around his palm. "I'm so sorry. I should have had my phone with me."

He shrugged. "Reception is sometimes spotty once you get away from the house. It might not have been any help. Your son, on the other hand, is one hell of a smart kid."

She might have taken offense at the "your son" reference, if not for the fact that Trent's face beamed with pride.

No mother could resist praise for her offspring. "He *is* pretty amazing," she said smugly. The she sobered. "I was terrified to let him go off on his own, but what choice did we have?"

"He took me right to you. He was a trooper."

The room fell silent. She was tremblingly aware of the fact that Trent stroked the back of her hand, almost absentmindedly.

He stood and reached forward to tuck a strand of hair behind her ear...then kissed her cheek. "Why did you turn down my marriage proposal, Bryn?" He propped one arm on the bed rail and stared at her intently.

She plucked at her IV nervously, unable to meet his eyes. "I'm able to provide for my son."

"That's not what I asked."

She slanted him a sideways gaze. "I didn't want to be an obligation to you...a wrong you have to right."

He frowned. "That doesn't even make sense. I offered to make you my wife."

"Like a business merger." She heard the petulance in her own voice and winced inwardly.

A smile began to draw up the corners of Trent's sensual mouth. "I may be good at a lot of things," he muttered, "but that was my first proposal. It possibly lacked finesse."

She pouted. "It lacked *something*."

He grinned fully now, picking up her hand and kissing each scrape. "Would it have helped if I told you I adore you...that I've loved you since you were a little girl in ragged shorts and scabbed-up knees. That what I felt for you changed over the years into something far deeper. But that I was too much of a self-centered, ego-driven jerk to recognize what I had before I lost it. That I need you so much it hurts, and I didn't even know there was anything missing in my life until you showed up in Wyoming."

Bryn lay, openmouthed, and thought her heart might break. For Trent, the self-contained, tightly controlled man that he was, to humble himself in such a way was a gift she had never expected. She was speechless.

His smile was wry. "Is that a second *no?*"

She gulped. "No. I mean yes. Oh, Trent, I

don't know what to say." She sniffed, blinking rapidly.

He shook his head and wiped her cheeks tenderly with the edge of the sheet. "You're killing me, little one. Any kind of answer would be appreciated. A man can only stand so much suspense."

She grabbed his hand in hers and squeezed. "Are you sure?" She couldn't bear it if he was confusing affection with love.

He kissed her again. Harder this time. With echoes of the passion they had shared. "Do I strike you as indecisive, Brynnie? *Yes*—I love you. And I promise you I'm not going to change my mind in five minutes or fifty years. So you might as well get used to it."

She tugged him closer. "Sit on the bed."

He lowered the bed rail and complied, but he pretended to look toward the hall with apprehension. "I'm scared of that nurse. Please don't get me in trouble."

She wanted to laugh, but her chest was a

huge bubble of happiness that made it hard to breathe.

He put an arm around her shoulders and settled her against his chest, her cheek over his beating heart. She decided there and then that a broken ankle was a small price to pay.

"Yes," she said with a soft sigh.

He kissed her temple. "Yes to what?"

"To everything. To laughter. To forever. I love you, Trent."

He stretched his long legs out on the mattress, one ankle propped over the other. "Are you sure?"

He was mocking her, but she was too happy to care. "I'm sure," she said, grinning uncontrollably. "So kiss your calm, ordered life goodbye."

He nuzzled the top of her head and sighed from deep in his chest. "I can't wait, Brynnie. I can't wait."

* * * * *